AF291362

A MASK
THE COLOUR
OF THE SKY

Bassem Khandaqji

A MASK
THE COLOUR
OF THE SKY

*Translated from the Arabic
by Addie Leak*

Europa
editions

Europa Editions
8 Blackstock Mews
London N4 2BT
www.europaeditions.co.uk

This book is a work of fiction. Any references to historical events,
real people, or real locales are used fictitiously.

A catalogue record for this title is available from the British Library
ISBN 978-1-78770-632-3

Khandaqji, Bassem
A Mask the Colour of the Sky

Cover design and illustration by Ginevra Rapisardi

Prepress by Grafica Punto Print – Rome

The authorized representative in the EEA
is Edizioni e/o, via Gabriele Camozzi 1, 00192 Rome, Italy.

Printed and bound in Great Britain by Clays Ltd, Elcograf S.p.A

C O N T E N T S

To my uncle Khalid, my earliest companion always,
And my aunt Nadia, ever the strong daughter
of the Al Yasmina Quarter

A MASK THE COLOUR OF THE SKY

Part I

Nur

I sang in order to feel the wasted horizon in
    the pain of a dove
not to explain what God says to man
I'm no prophet
I don't proclaim that my fall is an ascent.
—from *Mural*, by Mahmoud Darwish,
trans. Rema Hammami and John Berger

CHAPTER 1

[VOICE MEMO #12 – MONDAY, APRIL 19, 2021 – DAWN, SEVENTH DAY OF RAMADAN – NOTES FOR THE NOVEL]

For five-plus years now, I've been investigating Roman Palestine in the days of Jesus, trying desperately to uncover the true story of Mary Magdalene. Up to this point, I've failed miserably, but now—after a lot of frustration and a long break—I've decided I really can't let it go. I can't let anyone—not Dan Brown or all the Holy Grails clinked to toast *The Da Vinci Code*—take over her story with their nonsense and steal it from me. So I'm heading back into her world: its religion, its history, and all the secrets surrounding her. I'll dig up the notes I gathered for my research, which stalled for several reasons. The biggest challenge of them all? The faint, practically nonexistent presence of Magdalene in the historical record—both official and unsanctioned.

So yes, even though I'm bone-tired, run down, and feeling totally divorced from reality, I'm going to try and write a novel. I'll give it every ounce of imagination I have, then add more on top of that. In the end, that's all accepted history is, anyway: imagination, rationalized.

How should I write the novel, though? What style will I use?

And what should the title be? Will I even be able to publish it here, when publishing in this country's so anemic?

I've been spending a lot of time with novels and literary criticism lately, and it's made me a stronger writer, but to novelize

Magdalene's life, I need language that's both subtle and sturdy. I've been thinking about using two timelines, too: the historical past and the present, like Elif Shafak in *The Forty Rules of Love*. The style suits me, and I like the way it flows . . .

Then there's the characters. The main character in the present-day will be a university professor who studies antiquities. Or—no . . . that would be an obvious rip-off of Dan Brown and his novels. So let's make him a novelist. He wants to write a novel about Mary Magdalene, and he comes up with a story about a mysterious box holding a treasure, or some of her things. I don't know what kinds of things; I can figure that out later. Then this novelist has a series of adventures. He'll be from Haifa, Jaffa, or Nazareth—a great-grandson of Palestinians who stood firm on their land during the Nakba in '48. That way I can have him use his blue Israeli ID to visit all the archaeological sites scattered throughout the country. I'll throw in a main character who's a woman, too, to balance out the novelist. Wait—the novelist's name will be Naseem Shakr . . . It's a good name for a writer. And the female character is a journalist or historian . . . The novelist will be forty-two; it's a nice, mature age for a good-looking, unmarried guy . . . And the woman has been his friend since university; they disagreed when it came to getting married, so she got together with someone else but then separated from her husband, and now she's back with Naseem. Her name is Maram. She's so beautiful it hurts.

I'll have them make love a few times in the novel, to spice things up. But I'll be careful not to overuse sex . . . The point isn't obscenity or lust: I'm not trying to write a bodice-ripper, just add a little excitement.

In the other timeline, the one in the past, Mary Magdalene will be the main character, surrounded by disciples and apostles, especially Peter, John, and Levi . . . Oh, and it will take place after Jesus was crucified and first appeared to Mary Magdalene. I'll add in a fictional disciple for Mary, too, who will play a big role in the story: Simon the Lame, her main follower and a major part of her inner circle. I'll be sure to respect Christian religious sentiment, and I won't interrupt the narrative with too much historical, religious, or Gnostic information; I'd hate to alienate my readers, male and female alike, with too many facts. On the other hand, it would be good to get a better sense of what drives the book and think about it more in terms of the main character—what pushes him to embark on this journey? What challenges and obstacles will he face?

PS: Murad treats my research like a joke. It *really* bothers me . . .

He tapped his phone screen to stop recording the memo and checked the time. An hour and a half left to sleep before his morning appointment.

* * *

The Alleys

The alleyways of the refugee camp surrounded him, enveloped him, closing in tighter and tighter as he reluctantly hurried through them. Alleys were a bad way to start a morning, and today was no exception. Dew covered his aspirations like rust, corroding them as the thirty-something broke into a jog, rushing to get to his bleak morning appointment.

Nur Mahdi al-Shahdi sped up. He was a son of the camp. Of all the camps, really, because what difference did it make if it was this one or that one? They were all alike; what was the point of naming them at all? That's what he told himself in the privacy of his own mind, though not to the people around him. He'd favored silence from early on in a childhood spent in a cement alleyway, one he wasn't born and raised in, but born *from*.

The way he saw it, he'd come from the alley itself, from a womb hidden inside it that only the ill-fated souls born after the Nakba knew about; it was the first thing they saw as they filled their new lungs to scream. These were souls born well-versed in orphanhood—the bereaved, the injured, the silencer and the silenced, the wanderers and the estranged, all born ready and equipped with all of misery's armor, whether these particular alleys provided it or not. So what was the use of names?

The name of a Palestinian refugee camp meant nothing until a massacre was committed there. That made it one more line item on history's list of tragedies, a Tel al-Zaatar, Sabra or Shatila, Jenin or Al-Shati. As for his camp, no major massacre had taken place there yet, or not that people talked about. Which was also the difference between a refugee camp and a Jewish ghetto in Europe: the ability to create legend from tragedy and ensure that it would persist in the modern imagination. They'd made it the stuff of legends, engraved it into people's minds so effectively that it led to their creating this camp and forming the diaspora, gifting Nur and others like him with refugee status. Wasn't that what Elias Khoury was getting at in *Children of the Ghetto*? Nur glanced down at the plastic bag he held, which had two books inside it: *Fanon: The Postcolonial Imagination* by Nigel C. Gibson and Khoury's *Children of the Ghetto: My Name Is Adam*. He had another thought as he turned out of the last alleyway leading to Jerusalem Street, which stretched off toward the city of Al-Bireh. *In seventy years or so, I wonder what the ruins of this camp will say about the lengths we'll go to rationalize human cruelty. Maybe everything . . .*

As a scholar of history and archaeology, he wondered a lot about things like this. He had a degree in Islamic antiquities from the Higher Institute of Archaeology at Al-Quds University, and sometimes he wondered, bitterly, if he was really the only person in this entire camp of eight thousand refugees to attend the institute. *But what did the camp need with more ruins, anyway?*

Then there she was at the end of the alley, waiting for him, haloed, watching as he drew closer on that April morning that would flow into a Ramadan day, richer for her presence in it: an old woman, all patience and resilience. He drew closer, catching his breath, and bent to kiss her hand and wish her good morning. Her voice quavered, but her tone was compassionate and hopeful as she returned the greeting. "Good morning, Abu Nura."

Hearing her say his name—his nickname at that—always calmed and comforted him. He needed the warmth she gave off more than he could express. Hajja Fatima al-Musa, whom they also called Umm Adli after her eldest son, was sixty years old and had a face that resisted the effects of both time and the alleyways, remaining as bright and perfect as the full moon.

And why not? She was getting ready to visit another son, and her heart was brimming over with emotion. This son had been sentenced to life in prison, charged with planning and carrying out attacks against Occupation soldiers, and for ten years he'd been held in the depths of Zionist detention centers. He was her youngest son, Murad, and Nur's only friend in the world.

Nur looked at her for a moment before, together, they crossed the road leading to Al-Bireh, where the International Red Cross was headquartered. In front of it was the bus that would transport the prisoners' families to see their loved ones. It was a ten-minute walk with Umm Adli holding his arm the entire way, ten minutes for him to remember his own mother and his shared memories with Murad, and to get the blood flowing in her legs before she was tucked into the bus for eight hours—four there, four back. It was a journey she undertook year-round. Murad had described it in his letters. "She makes this trip winter and summer, Nur; she's never too tired or hopeless to come. All just to see me for for-ty-five minutes a month (max!) from behind a glass barrier that muffles all feeling. If you don't count the times the Occupation shuts things down for 'security reasons' on national or religious holidays, I only get to see my mother for 450 minutes a year. If I'm lucky. There are some holidays, friend, that we celebrate— or pretend to—and then there are others that are celebrated at our expense, on our time. That's what the Occupation's plotting, slowly but surely: the death of time. On holidays, the soldiers lock us in a temporality outside their own until they finish their prayers and rituals, then release us for a little while into a time, into a dimension, that has nothing to do with the outer world. It's another temporality altogether, and it's jarring."

Nur inspected Umm Adli carefully, asking after her health and if she'd had a nice meal for suhoor before the day's fast began. Thinking of the coronavirus pandemic, he also asked if her surgical mask was new and if she had a good alcohol-based hand sanitizer with her. She responded yes to both questions, leaning on his shoulder and praising God for getting her the vaccine so she could visit Murad.

Soon, Hajja Umm Adli would board the bus alone and head off to visit her son, but for the rest of those ten minutes, the length of their walk, Nur wasn't afraid of the onslaught of memory.

It besieged him, penetrated him, danced a tango with him, two steps back, one to the side, over and over. And he goaded it with his usual silence, that mad silence he'd cultivated from an early age in the folds of a miserable family that had mastered it.

His thoughts wrested him from those morning moments to a Ramadan evening in mid-August 2011. He and Murad had been wandering through the winding alleyways of the camp's souq, idling away the few moments left before the evening call to prayer and then iftar. Murad had invited Nur to a fancy Ramadan banquet, its table groaning beneath the weight of his favorite dish, waraq enab, its broad grape leaves stuffed with rice and lamb. They made their way to Umm Adli's house, throats parched in August's scorching heat, as the streets gradually emptied out, everyone heading home to break the fast. The invitation had been a special one to celebrate Nur finally enrolling in college, after more than two years of working himself to the bone to save up.

"Can't you find something to major in besides history and archaeology?" Murad asked, a little derisively.

Nur chose to ignore his tone. "Nothing else speaks to me."

Murad was well aware that this discussion with Nur wouldn't go far. Given Nur's short breaths and clipped answers, it was clearly destined to end in dignified silence.

Murad, like his friend, dreamed of enrolling in college, but he wanted to become a skilled lawyer, one with good judgment and a moral compass. His silver tongue would be an asset in the field, especially when coupled with his bold manner and ability to let fly the perfect barb in the most trying circumstances. As for Nur, his love of history and archaeology was kindled when a Palestinian labor contractor from occupied Jerusalem got him a two-week job at a site west of the city, where an American university was excavating. His assignment had been to transport and sift soil.

That's when he was touched by a passion for the earth, when he came across the mysteries it contained: pieces of pottery, seals, figurines, and coins, all buried in the soil for thousands of years. The earth touched him with its revelations, the earth that only babbled its secrets to those who caressed it with expert fingers, gently, patiently, stubbornly tickling it till it trembled and cried out.

Before they dove into the last alleyway leading to his house, Murad asked again, this time with eyebrows raised: "And of course, your father's happy with your decision, right? To pick those majors?"

Nur turned to him more sharply this time—Murad's question stinging him out of his silence—but he responded calmly, his posture relaxing: "I don't know if he'd be happy if I told him."

Murad whistled in astonishment mixed with disdain: "You still haven't told him?"

But before Nur could answer, the disaster occurred. It had been planned to a T by a special unit of the Zionist Occupation army, some of its members disguising themselves as women, and it happened at lightning speed. Rough hands snatched Murad from his conversation with Nur, from the alleyways of the camp, from his home, his youth, his memories, and his mother's table embellished with grape leaves. In the blink of an eye, they took him. He disappeared out from under Nur's nose as he stood startled and silent, gasping for air. What had happened didn't sink in until, cowering in a narrow cement alleyway, he heard the boom of stun grenades and the whizzing of bullets that masked his lifelong friend's kidnapping, then the wailing of Umm Adli, who, moments before, had been balancing plates of delicious food.

Since that disastrous night, Nur had stopped fasting during Ramadan, devoting himself instead to silence, and Umm Adli had stopped preparing grape leaves in her kitchen. Umm Adli, who now interrupted the dance of his memory by asking the question she never tired of, "When will they let Murad out, so I can throw you a double wedding?"

"Soon, Khalti . . . soon," he answered, feigning hope and optimism.

Then, as usual, she began to pray fervently for the soul of Nur's mother, Noura Karadneh, who bled out after giving birth to him at no more than twenty years old. In a cruel twist of fate, neither her young age nor the fact that he was her first child could save her. Hajja Umm Adli sang of Noura's beauty, the blueness of her eyes and blondeness of her hair, her pale skin and grace, her beauty marks and freckles . . . "Your mother was the sun and moon of Al-Lydd, the most beautiful girl in the neighborhood." He hadn't inherited her memories but did inherit her paleness and the blue of her eyes, as well as long, curly hair that shifted in colour from brown to sandy blonde. From his father, he'd gotten a thick beard shot through with red and a tall, slender frame.

It was this appearance, coupled with his charm, that gave him, or perhaps cursed him with, multiple nicknames that echoed in the camp's alleyways. Abu Nura, Ajnabi or "foreigner," American, and Saknaji, which they used for fair-haired Jews. He held tightly to the bag in his hand, banishing the echoes of that last epithet from his mind. In one of the books inside the bag was a letter Nur was smuggling to Murad, tiny words written between the lines of text in light pencil, so the warden wouldn't see them during his inspection of incoming books. Murad had taught him to write letters this way when he started using the book swap during the monthly visits to exchange secret messages. Murad had made good use of his suffering in detention, as well, transforming his time there into a path toward knowledge and erudition that would lead him to freedom, at least on the inside.

In one of his letters to Nur, he wrote, "'Prison is density.' That's what Mahmoud Darwish said into the emptiness of his first cell as he sat there longing for his mother's coffee and bread . . . But I didn't really get it until I grew a backbone in detention."

That density eventually led him to sign up for the bachelor's degree program for prisoners of the Zionist Occupation, and later graduate with a degree in political science. Several years later, he followed it with a master's degree in Israeli studies from Al-Quds University's graduate school.

Murad faced the metal bars of detention with an iron will, and he beat back the bitterness of exile with the hope flowing from his pen, which he used to combat deprivation and the acute, systematic uprooting of humanity from its time and place. Murad was possessed by this density to the point that he'd reproached Nur in his last letter for being so preoccupied with Mary Magdalene that he was neglecting to engage with contemporary issues that needed research. Murad judged things from his own perspective—and why not? He was doing his own research about the colonial structure of the Zionist regime. He wanted his friend to join him in confronting the narrative and intellectual limitations of the Occupation. Little did he realize that he was the one who'd first ignited this passion for Mary Magdalene in Nur's chest when, several years prior, he'd asked him for Dan Brown's *Da Vinci Code* and *The Holy Blood and the Holy Grail* by Michael Baigent. Nur had a tendency to read most of the books Murad asked him for, including books and studies on the Zionist entity, and Murad knew he'd watched the *Da Vinci Code* film starring Tom Hanks, but the text had fired him up even more, setting him on the trail of the real Magdalene. After all, wasn't he a researcher, with history and archaeology coursing through his veins? Hadn't his thesis been a careful study of the Bar Kokhba Revolt, which took place in the Roman era, a century after Christ's crucifixion?

He was thrilled by the imagination's mighty ability to topple history from its pedestal of truth and rationality. Was Dan Brown imagining history or was he cheating it? What had he done to Mary Magdalene? What had he done to Nur that pushed him to research Magdalene for five years? And why would a foreign writer uproot Mary Magdalene from her historical Palestinian context to throw her into the abyss of the West? Why?

The bus appeared in the distance, white against the quiet morning, waiting for them. The streets of Ramallah and Al-Bireh were empty except for the families of prisoners who'd shaken off the long, wakeful Ramadan night, their drowsiness and fatigue, to head, with all their self-sacrifice and longing, to the Occupation prisons where they would visit their sons and daughters. There were only those families and Umm Adli's heavy breathing, and just five minutes left until they reached the bus. He turned to her, looked at her carefully, looked at her face, always as bright as the full moon before and during her visit with Murad. When she returned, burdened with grief and loss, it would be as though the moon had been eclipsed.

He looked away from her to ease the tightness in his chest, recalling the letter he'd written to Murad the night before:

Do you really have a problem with my work on Magdalene, Murad? Are you saying I prefer being lost in vague historical labyrinths to facing the facts of everyday life? That I'm an escapist?

You can be so harsh sometimes!

You're the one who told me, in your last letter, that colonialism was in the details; it's an obsession with control and all the little things that, put together, form a comprehensive, integrated structure. Details of history, culture, psychology, and knowledge. That's why we have to fight it with the same details.

Isn't the story of Mary Magdalene one of those?

Isn't the Orientalism you're trying to pin on me the same thing that destroyed Magdalene's voice in our country, making her recite, supplicate, and pray in Latin, Greek, and Old French?

And isn't it my right to try and restore it with my research, however trivial I, and my place in society, might be?

At any rate, my friend, let me tell you, with the heaviest of hearts, that I've failed. But I'm pleased to announce that I've decided to turn the research into a novel. I'll send more details soon, but I'm planning to take some of your criticism to heart, which means that part of the novel will be set in the present—at least if you promise to stop accusing me of escapism. The truth is, I'm completely entangled in our reality. I work within it on a daily basis . . . In Jerusalem, Murad, I drink in lies and myths that have been manipulated to the core; I drink them in, then spit them back out with everything I've got. Since our Nakba, at least, we've been the victims of a massive assault—and I want to face it head on . . . "

The bus was monstrous and white, and it was as though he were seeing it for the first time. He helped Umm Adli climb aboard and seated her beside the window, where she could see the ruins of Al-Lydd as the bus made its way to the desert prison of Nafha in the southern Negev. Then he kissed her forehead and sent his warm greetings to Murad, promising to wait for her at the bus stop when she got back that evening. That way, he could check in on her and receive his own share of news and secret messages from his friend.

He began the walk back to the camp. To the alleyways. To the miserable house, in a morning that refused to pass, stubbornly lingering instead, a stage for the memory that was now running riot over it. A time when he was the only one to decide whether the way back would take ten minutes of his meaningless day or more.

The way back to the camp was still desolate. He was the sort of refugee who didn't truly feel the camp until he left it and was immediately labeled as just that: a refugee, no more, no less. Down in the winding alleys, that's not what he was, or at least there was no one there to remind him of it because everyone in the camp was similar, with the same names. In this big concrete city of Ramallah/Al-Bireh, though (or Al-Bireh/Ramallah), he was a refugee, even if neither his face nor his frame gave him away. His Otherness in this city and its artificial, disordered, occupied squares and streets was enough.

There was only Jerusalem. When he breathed in her air, the Otherness would begin to dissolve, little by little, until he could soar in her space. It was a love affair, the thing that brought him together with the city; he would glorify her names in poems, songs, and prayers. She was the only one who had compassion for him, hiding him in her folds and ancient houses in his darkest moments. Ramallah wasn't like that; his relationship with that city was one of words, explosions, and vomit, all of which felt interchangeable.

He made his way down the sidewalk in the shade of the residential and commercial buildings that had been haphazardly planned and built along the street. The piles of rock and iron and cement suffocated him. He turned to his left, where the massive City Inn stood, stopped walking for a few moments to contemplate its façade, and then smiled sadly; he used to work there, in the hotel's lobbies, corridors, guest rooms, and restaurant, doing night shifts in college, before he graduated and started work as a tour guide at a Jerusalem travel agency.

To cover his university fees and living expenses, he would study one semester and skip the next. This made it possible for him to get a bachelor's degree in around seven years, twice the usual time. The skipped semesters he spent toiling at construction sites and cleaning houses and office buildings in the depths of the Zionist entity. The work provided him with what he needed to pay his eye-watering university fees and contribute to the finances of his small, bereft family. When he was enrolled at university and his savings ran out, he would resort to working as a waiter at the City Inn. There, according to the HR director's words of encouragement one shift, he was basically the ideal employee: "A good-looking college kid who speaks fluent English . . . polite and quiet . . . you're the perfect waiter at the perfect hotel!"

At that hotel, Nur had witnessed events, lives, and destinies file fleetingly past him. Deed and happenstance, love and desire.

Nur Mahdi al-Shahdi was no prude, but casual sex and illicit sexuality frightened him. He ran from them and repelled all offers, instead venting the lava of his lust through his secret habit (as they say), making love to the entire hotel in the most explicit fantasies.

His bumpy road at uni was no different from his work at the hotel; life as a student wasn't adorned with any love story, consummated or no. In short, he was irreparably damaged, a wreck on the inside, saturated with chastity, fear, and maybe stupidity. At least that's how his colleagues at the hotel described him: a dumbass . . . *Imagine! A good-looking kid like you, saying no to comfort and pleasure. What an idiot!*

An idiot who isolated himself with silence and hard work, a waiter par excellence, guaranteed a modest salary boosted by tips that allowed him to maintain his style and his extravagant spending habits when it came to clothing, shoes, and colognes. If he was an idiot, this was where the screw was loose. He may have been a poor, miserable refugee, but he took pride in possessing a certain desirable elegance. That elevated sense of style went all too well with his self-destruction and silence, and his retreat into his shell. Was Murad right, then, when he accused him of being an escapist? Maybe it was true: he had neither the strength nor the courage to face reality in all its gritty detail.

As he walked, an idea for the novel on Mary Magdalene

began to take shape in his mind; he would record it using the voice memo app on his phone as soon as he got home. All at once, he was propelled forward, as if a fierce wind had suddenly filled his sails, rushing him toward the entrance of the camp, to the right of which was parked a metal cart carrying a large box with a glass display window set into it, secured with an old lock and an iron chain. It was a sad-looking cart that he was tempted to smash, iron or no iron—his father's cart, which he, in turn, had inherited from *his* father, Rashid al-Shahdi, who'd owned a café in the vegetable souq in Al-Lydd pre-Nakba. Al-Lydd, which Nur had never entered as a returnee but, instead, as a laborer in its workshops and souqs, where he'd never come upon the slightest whiff of where his grandfather's café had been. His grandfather, meanwhile, had become a lonely man, doomed by this cart that Nur was now tearing to pieces with his eyes.

As a child, he'd stood right there behind the cart next to his father, helping him distribute hot drinks and juices to customers: laborers, passersby, and shopkeepers in the camp's souq.

No sooner had his father, Mahdi, been released from the Occupation prisons in the late winter of '95 than the scales of his mind went askew, growing heavier, or possibly lighter. They asked him, "What will you do now that the Intifada has faded, peace has been made, and we've got a Palestinian 'Authority'?" Nobody knows what came over him, but he responded hoarsely, answering his mother, Sumayyah; the camp and the alleyways; his little boy; and the graves of his father and his wife Noura: "Ahwa wa shai."

Then Sumayyah, fondly called Umm Mahdi, exploded at her only son, slipped off her shoe, and slapped her face with it: "Have you completely lost your mind, Mahdi? Are you giving up on the struggle after everything you went through in prison? After how proud your father—God have mercy on him—was of you? You're going to give it all up to start a tea and coffee stand?"

"Coffee and tea, Immi . . . Coffee and tea and sahlab."

As for Nur, he didn't recognize this new father who'd come from the darkness of detention five years after he'd been born and then orphaned by the tragedy of his mother, Noura. He didn't hate his father, but he did hate coffee and tea. Without knowing it, he'd inherited his father's silence, disillusionment, and inscrutable ways.

He approached the cart now and examined it, then ran his hand along it. Chained and rusty, it resembled his father as it sat there, locked tightly and fettered on this Ramadan morning. Fettered like his father, who was at that moment fast asleep inside his house, tucked away deep within the camp, and who would open the cart after iftar to prepare coffee and tea, then remain open until suhoor time without getting tired or desperate or uttering a single word more or less than was necessary. He would respond to customers in a mumble, a lit cigarette perpetually dangling from lips set into the thick gray beard of a man a little over fifty.

It didn't make much difference to Nur whether his father was standing behind the cart now or not; the mumble was the same, the silence the same. The only thing that ever differed was the intensity of his looks and their disappointment-laced sorrow.

Nur sighed, then plunged into the alleys.

* * *

He slipped inside the house surrounded by a thousand alleyways and enveloped in a darkness in keeping with its quiet and melancholy air. A swarm of curses wound their way around this single-story home with its small rooftop room, which was Nur's sanctuary and shelter when he wanted to escape the mood in the house. At the moment, the space was dominated by his father's thunderous snores, coming from his bedroom at the end of the hall. Nur wondered the same thing he always did: *How on earth has Khadija put up with the racket all these years?*

He headed for the kitchen like a stray dog looking for crumbs to silence its howling stomach, then up to his little room, padding along quietly so that Khadija wouldn't wake up from her own majestic snores and snap at him for disturbing her dreams.

She was fifty years old and both his father's wife and his aunt—his mother's sister. His father had married her a year after he was released from prison in accordance with the wishes of his late mother, Sumayyah, who hoped that he would be cured of the mad fit that had provoked his silence and his venture with the coffee and tea cart. She hoped, too, that this move would break the jinx on the Al-Shahdi family, which was on the verge of dying out due to its failure to sprout new branches on the family tree. Mahdi was his father's only child, and Nur emerged into the light without deviating from that rule of oneness. His grandmother's hopes for him to have more offspring and grow the clan were shattered by Khadija's rocky womb and the death of desire in her only son's heart.

Khadija didn't have a child despite the grandmother's many interventions, which ran the gamut from folk wisdom and magic to medicine and religion. No child for the widow, the widow of Mahdi's friend Firas, who had been martyred just a month after marrying Khadija at the height of the Stone Intifada in 1988. The martyr's widow had great hopes then that the martyr's friend Mahdi would marry her, but he had already won Noura and all of her beauty and charm.

But Khadija's hopes of marrying Mahdi were later revived, and that's exactly what she did. She became the wife of both the martyr and the freed prisoner, the wife who never had and never would have children from either of the two heroes. Firas wasn't the only one who was killed and fell a martyr; when a heart falls prey to tragedy, it can become a living martyr to love and longing.

That's what happened to Mahdi al-Shahdi; he became a sort of martyr the moment he received news of Noura's death.

But that wasn't the only thing that shattered his illusions and made his heart wither in his chest. There was also the all-encompassing, ungrateful disownment of his small family—his mother and his orphan child—during the years he was detained. He was unjustly sentenced to twenty-five years in prison, of which he served five, during which time he was dealt this second blow by his friends and comrades in the Intifada, all busy with their new stateliness, which indulged in a shameless dance with the Authority of Delusion and Confusion and the unsettled peace. They stopped caring for his family. Making things even worse, his enemies and captors required him, before his release, to sign a pledge like every other released prisoner, a pledge to renounce violence and respect the terms of the Oslo Accords between the Palestinian Liberation Organization and the Zionist entity. His revolutionary spirit was broken.

Mahdi al-Shahdi, hero of the Intifada and master of the camp's alleyways, the wanted man who gave his enemies lessons in resistance, saw his struggle rechristened "violence" and his revolution "terrorism." As for the suffering that sprang from being arrested and prevented from supporting his wife, the love of his life, in her dying days, or from helping his tormented mother or his parentless child, all of it became idle chatter on the rubbish heap in his mind. Mahdi signed the pledge not to return to violence and felt that he'd thrown his soul into a bottomless pit of disillusionment, returning from detention as though from the horrors of hell, his eyes hollow and wandering, his hair matted, and his protruding bones accompanied by a hoarseness that suggested that he hadn't been struck dumb in prison but, rather, been struck by an oppressive silence and overwhelming loss. "Ahwa wa shai," he said to his mother at a time when his name still shook the camp with memories of his glorious past in the Intifada. He tried not to think of the way his erstwhile friends and former comrades had collected to themselves high-ranking positions, caviar, cigars, and fast cars. They became civil servants, accountable to the people, while he ceased to be accountable to anything but the tea and coffee cart. The people of the camp were astonished. Some were convinced that Mahdi al-Shahdi had gone mad in prison and not yet recovered fully enough to decide how to turn his struggle to his advantage, as others had. Many camp residents, however, respected him more, appreciating that he didn't sully his blood with opportunism or cash in on the struggle's legacy.

Sumayyah revealed the secret of this disillusionment to Khadija. Khadija revealed the secret to Nur and then went silent. Nur swallowed the secret and went silent as well. The whole house was silent.

He sat on the edge of the bed inside his cluttered little room, which had no hope of becoming either organized or charming. There were wooden shelves piled high with books, some new and others worn, folders and notebooks scattered chaotically about. In the corners of the room lay pieces of pottery and ancient oil lamps he'd come across during the archaeological digs he'd participated in since university; he'd received them as mementos, either openly or in secret, as a reward for his skill in excavating.

He pulled his phone out of his pocket, maintaining his daily morning habit of browsing through different online newspapers and archaeology sites. He went to a Palestinian news site and quickly scanned the headlines.

Occupation Forces Attack Farmers in North Jordan Valley

Jerusalem Citizen Must Pay to Demolish His Own Home: Occupation Claims Lack of Permit

Palestinian Leadership Prepares for Legislative Elections

Coronavirus Cases Decline

Parliamentary Election Results Have Not Yet Decided Israel's Next Government

AS TENSIONS RISE, OCCUPATION ANNOUNCES INTENTION TO EVICT SHEIKH JARRAH RESIDENTS

And that was quite enough for Occupation news. He snorted. *Apparently the Occupation is part of daily life now . . . just totally normal. This must be what Murad means by "the small colonial details"!*

Then he switched from the news to another page specializing in history and archaeology, looking for any new information regarding Mary Magdalene that might dazzle him, but he didn't find anything.

He closed the page, withdrawing from the temptations of the internet, and opened the voice memos app. After clearing his throat, he spoke solemnly, shaking off the wild storms of memory that had been overwhelming him since morning:

[VOICE MEMO #13 – MONDAY MORNING, 19 APRIL 2021 / 7 RAMADAN – INITIAL THOUGHTS ON THE NOVEL]

My knowledge base about the Bar Kokhba Revolt of 132-136 AD should give me one of the main frameworks I need for the historical side of the novel. As for the general concept, I have a few initial thoughts.

First, maybe there's a buried treasure having something to do with Mary Magdalene. Either in her village, Magdala, on the west bank of Lake Tiberias, or in the church dedicated to her on the Mount of Olives. The treasure would be some sort of ivory box or trunk containing statuettes of Magdalene's seven demons or a vial of the expensive nard perfume she poured on Jesus. The trunk might also contain locks of her hair, which she used to wipe Jesus's feet dry. The statues would have been carved by a Roman sculptor who secretly converted to Christianity, and when he died, he would've left them to his children and grandchildren, who kept them a secret for fear of oppression from the Jewish and Roman leaders in Jerusalem. Then the Bar Kokhba Revolt led to Jerusalem's destruction and the killing of the Jews and their expulsion, so the sculptor's family migrated from Jerusalem to the north. They settled, as other families did, beside the Roman base of the Sixth "Ironclad" Legion on the Plain of Megiddo, which was Palestine's northern border back then and is known today as Tel Megiddo or Wadi al-Lajjun. The family's decision to take refuge there came from their dread of the Jews regaining control or returning to Jerusalem. To protect the statuettes from being lost or stolen, one of the sculptor's grandchildren resorted to a magic charm, a sort of talisman he used to keep an eye on the seven demons and protect the box when he hid it inside a secret rock beneath his house.

Problems with this concept:

It's weak, and Magdalene herself isn't part of it. And then, what's the point of carving the statuettes? And when would the story take place? Past or present? What role would Naseem and Maram play?

PS: Umm Adli cut me to the quick this morning on the way to the bus; with every breath, she exhaled maternal tenderness . . . She cut me to the quick without even realizing she was sacrificing me to my memories, which are still eating away at me . . .

He stopped recording with a grumble of frustration, gazing down at the phone in his hands for several moments before he turned toward the heavy mirror on the wall in front of him and stared at his face as though discovering it for the first time. Then he collapsed onto the bed, pulled by his exhaustion into slumber.

* * *

Nur Mahdi al-Shahdi wasn't born just once, but several times throughout the years of his life in the alleys.

The first was on April 1, 1991, when he lived and his mother Noura died, along with her twenty years of age, her golden curls, and the sun of Al-Lydd, which was eclipsed when his father was arrested just weeks after his wedding only to return from captivity five years later broken, betrayed, and bewildered, silent and silenced.

Nur was born a second time from his father's silence and his tea and coffee cart, and he took refuge in his grandmother Sumayyah, who raised and nurtured him on stories of Al-Lydd and his mother Noura. That was until Sumayyah died or, rather, decided to die on the fiftieth anniversary of the Nakba, her efforts to produce descendants and strengthen her family tree having failed. Mahdi and Khadija had been struck by drought, and their bed was dry and desiccated, waterless down to its depths.

Nur was born the third time when his grandmother died and he was trained, whisper by whisper, in his father's silence in the still house where, some nights, he would awake to sobs and whimpers spilling from either his father or his father's wife.

An ensuing birth coincided with his fast friendship with Murad, who relieved his seclusion and silence throughout their shared childhood, until Murad was arrested and Nur began, once again, to worship at the altar of silence.

There was yet another birth, maybe the most painful and decisive he'd experienced, and that was after he passed his secondary school exams with distinction, only to enter the workforce rather than university. It was a C-section birth, his father the surgeon cutting into his chest and tampering with his heart in a rare blatant intervention in Nur's future.

Nur, who'd seen his distinction as an opportunity to extricate himself from the abyss of his father's silence and their disordered and repressed relationship, now feared that his destiny would resemble his father's, especially when he realized, in a later stage of the family's ill-fated and silent lives as refugees, that with his stillness and his reliance on him, his father had been isolating him from the alleyways and the camp. At the least, Nur's childhood was a far cry from that of Murad and his buddies, who wandered the alleys freely, throwing stones at the Occupation forces during their incursions into the camp and their periodic, violent raids and arrests.

Mahdi would close the doors and windows of the house, pulling Nur out of the alleys and throwing him into his room without the least comment or remark, just his usual scowl. He didn't shout at or scold Nur, and he didn't beat him, not even once. His only whip was the silence with which he lashed his son until his joy over his high marks faded. Then Mahdi calmly announced his absolute rejection of the financial aid offered by the Camp Services Committee, which was reserved for only the best students. By rejecting the handout, Mahdi was refusing to be ensnared by a scholarship that would have freed Nur from the financial burden of university and allowed him to live the life he dreamed of, maybe even flee the gloom of his house and his father's many tragedies.

This blatant intervention by his father was a rare and sparing pronouncement that left Nur no clues as to the reasoning behind it. Only Khadija, sensing one night that Nur was upset and on the verge of losing his mind, revealed one source of her husband's despair to him, whispering it in his ear: "They stabbed your father in the back . . . abandoned him and your mother and grandmother while he was in detention. And now they're trying to atone for their sins through you. They want to rope him back in."

"Who are 'they'?"

"The others like him. But they came down from the mountaintop, as he puts it."

"What mountaintop? There aren't any mountains in the camp."

"Oh, but there are . . . "

Working the tea and coffee cart wasn't enough to cover

Nur's tuition and the rest of his university bills. Mahdi didn't feel guilty; he was sure there was a will burning inside his son that would take him to university sooner or later. Then came the cruel hour of Nur's birth from the flanks of the Other's time, that era layered over his own face and identity, a birth so painful that it forced him into isolation from his work in Jerusalem and from the world for a month and a half.

He suffered the labor pangs that preceded this birth when the paths of suffering opened their gates to him and he walked down them alongside Murad, the two of them working as laborers in Jerusalem, Tel Aviv, and Al-Lydd, as well as many other parts of the Zionist entity. Nur worked in construction, painting, portering, cleaning, and gardening, and on archaeological digs. He toiled for two years to earn enough to launch his university career.

At work, Nur discovered his looks and began to recognize the privileges of the nickname the camp boys used to yell after him; in Tel Aviv, "Saknaji" became "Ashkenazi." The nickname demanded a language of its own, and the language was Hebrew, which he began to grasp little by little, gathering up single words, questions, and inquiries that he used to hound his colleagues at work who had mastered Hebrew. Just a few words at first. A commonplace expression here and there that resembled in pronunciation and meaning its Arabic equivalent. He would rush toward this other language and pounce on it. It's what he always did when he had his sights set on a certain goal; he would become afflicted with a passion that reached the point of obsession. So he bought books to learn Hebrew and listened to news broadcasts and songs in the language, watched Hebrew films. He took to it with diligence, not love; as he described it to Murad in a letter, it was a guttural language, the language of *kha*, but—perhaps to protect himself from those who spoke it—he caked his features with it. His Ashkenazi features! Hebrew became a "spoil of war" to be acquired, as Kateb

Yacine described French in colonial Algeria. But the difference between Kateb Yacine and Nur al-Shahdi was that the latter didn't learn Hebrew from the "mouth of the wolf" and Hebrew schools. He learned it from the Hebrew-speaking streets.

Arabic was the language of his heart, English the language of his mind, and Hebrew the language of his shadow side and his Ashkenazi features. Thus his face became a mask he put on when he sold his labor in Zionist marketplaces and squares, feeling the fatigue of earning a good wage, which he wouldn't have gotten around Ramallah. He didn't feel the enormous contradiction between his grandmother's stories about Al-Lydd and his work there as a laborer, rather than a returning refugee.

The first time he discovered the advantages of his features was when a Zionist police force raided a construction site he was working on with Murad and some others in the Rishon LeZion settlement north of Tel Aviv, the largest Zionist colonial settlement. The police were there to check the workers' permits and IDs and apprehend anyone working illegally, and Nur was among those unfortunate Palestinians denied work permits for the Zionist market, either due to previous arrests for resisting the Occupation or because a relative had been arrested. In Nur's case, he was held accountable for his father's offense. That day, however, he had a rare stroke of luck. He was relieving himself in a far-off corner of the site when the commotion started, and he saw the police surrounding the site and checking the workers' IDs. A wave of confused indecision washed over him as he looked around for some life raft that would protect him from the officers' blows and several days of detention at the station, followed by being tossed out on his head at the nearest border checkpoint between the occupied West Bank and the center of the Zionist world. But Nur couldn't see a way out, so he headed to turn himself in to the police, who were absorbed in their security duties. He walked up to them with what remained of his calm, confidence, and composure. He was about to stop and surrender himself to their fists when a policeman turned toward him at random, briefly examined his face, then greeted him in Hebrew and turned to check another laborer's work permit, not suspecting for a second that Nur was classified as a refugee, an "illegal," or a "laborer from the Palestinian territories." No sooner had Nur put some distance between himself and the construction site and police custody than he took off like the wind. He didn't return east, where the road led to Ramallah, but instead went west, toward the sea, toward Jaffa, the Bride of Palestine, and paced the shore as her groom, intoxicated by his small, wily victory over the police.

It was the features, then.

His features were a mask. He whooped. Danced. Dove into the sea. He was alone on the beach at Jaffa, and it was winter, and by the time Nur got back to Ramallah that evening, and then to his camp, he could no longer remember—had he been shouting in Arabic or Hebrew? The question lingered in his mind as he and Murad celebrated his lucky escape from the police.

The labor pains of this final, definitive birth had become more violent one autumn day three years ago as he wandered through Jaffa's famous flea market. He was immersed in contemplating the wares displayed on the carts and in the shops— old, dilapidated antiques; paintings; outdated appliances; and more—fascinated by the past and their accumulated history, trying to imagine the fates of their previous owners. Then, in the hustle and bustle of the souq, his gaze fell on a dark brown leather jacket hanging on a rack of used clothing in front of a shop. He crossed over to it quickly, drawn by how handsome it was. He examined it with the skill and expertise of someone with a weakness for stylish things and confirmed that it was real leather. He took it off the hanger and tried it on, studying his appearance in the shop mirror and admiring the leather. He decided to buy it. He went to the shopkeeper and began bargaining for the jacket in his Ashkenazi-accented Hebrew, finally reaching the reasonable price of fifty dollars. Then he left the souq in the jacket, happy in all his leather-clad Ashkenazi glory.

He stuck his hands in the jacket pockets as he made his way toward the central bus station to head back to Jerusalem, where his tour agency was headquartered. Then he began to rummage through the other pockets, and when he reached into the inner chest pocket over his heart, his fingers brushed against something. He pulled it out with eager curiosity. It was a blue Israeli ID card, intact, which the jacket's owner had apparently forgotten about when he sold the jacket at the market. Nur stopped in his tracks, looking around nervously—the knee-jerk reaction of an Arab refugee, despite the features protecting him from the scorching sun of Zionist Tel Aviv. There were some people passing nearby, so he walked slowly toward a wooden bench by the sidewalk, shaded from the sun and prying eyes by the thick foliage of a tree. He looked around again; everything was calm, life proceeding as usual, nothing to worry about. He took the card out of his pocket and flipped opened the plastic casing, looking at the owner's information and picture, from which a handsome young man gazed back at him.

FIRST NAME: OR
LAST NAME: SHAPIRA
MOTHER'S NAME: LITAL
FATHER'S NAME: NITZAN
BIRTH DATE: 15/8/1985
PLACE OF RESIDENCE: TEL AVIV

The owner of the card was five years older than he was. Or Shapira . . .

He was struck by the name: in Hebrew, *or* meant "light," just like *nur* in Arabic. A slight smile spread over Nur's face as he gazed at the ID; then he tucked it back into his inner jacket pocket, resting against his heart. And turned his steps back toward the camp.

* * *

He woke up just as the afternoon was starting to wane and tossed a bit in bed before yawning and rubbing his face with both hands, trying to snap himself out of remembered horrors. After drinking some water to make his voice less hoarse, he pressed "record":

"Voice memo # . . . "

But he'd forgotten the number of the last memo, so he decided on an impulse to stop numbering them and just make do with dates and titles. He sighed, then took a deep breath before he began recording again.

[MONDAY NIGHT, APRIL 19: ANOTHER CONCEPT
FOR THE MAGDALENE STORY]

I recently found out that the books of Acts and Revelation were written before the four Gospels. It's worth mentioning that according to John in Revelation, when Jesus comes back, his final battle against Satan and the forces of evil will take place on the Plain of Megiddo, also known as Harmagedōn—that is, Armageddon. So if I want to link Magdalene and her treasure to northern Palestine, it has to be based on Revelation. The family of the sculptor, or secret follower of Mary Magdalene, has to move to Tel Megiddo, and then stay there, because of an injunction passed down through generations requiring them to bury Magdalene's box, which contains not just the locks of her hair and her perfume but also her secret gospel, or maybe the location of her tomb. Then they must keep watch over it until Jesus comes down to resurrect her and be once again anointed by her perfume and wiped dry with her hair. This premise would need to be supported by contemporary events, such as the discovery of a leather-bound scroll at the Magdala village excavation site, or inscriptions that include riddles indicating the box's location. No . . . nope, I don't like this concept. There's something missing . . .

PS: When Murad recommended that I read Elias Khoury's *Children of the Ghetto*, I researched the origin of the name and the meaning of the word "ghetto" and was surprised to find out it was originally the name of a cannon-making foundry in Venice, Italy, next to which a Jewish community settled in 1516. It became common to say that the Jews lived next to the ghetto and, with time, that they lived in the ghetto. But what if the name of the foundry had been something like Paolo or Antonio? Would the Jews have lived in the paolo or the antonio? Would Elias Khoury have called his novel *Children of the Antonio*?

* * *

Shortly before the sundown call to prayer that heralded the breaking of the fast, Nur reached the Red Cross headquarters in Al-Bireh, where Hajja Umm Adli was just about to climb into her son Adli's car after the grueling return trip from her visit with Murad. He hurried toward them, suppressing his sorrow when he noticed how haggard she looked, the way bidding farewell to Murad until their next visit had eclipsed the moon that had been so bright and full in the morning. He drew level with her and kissed her head, trying to console her; then he reluctantly shook hands with Adli, exchanging hasty, superficial greetings. After she passed on Murad's greetings and well wishes, she gave him a bag that contained two books he'd sent. Nur bid her farewell, kissing her head again, and returned home, this time without any memories to slow him down or temper his eagerness to read the smuggled letter from Murad.

He stepped into the house and was met with a scene straight out of a silent, black-and-white film starring his father and Khadija, who were sitting in wordless gloom at the iftar table, lost in thought as they waited for the call to prayer to sound from the loudspeakers of the camp mosque's minaret. He launched a cursory greeting and continued up to his room without lingering or being invited to join them for the meal, leaving behind him an indifference stuffed to bursting with silence.

He sat on the edge of the bed and pulled the two books out of the bag eagerly. The first was *Life Is Negotiations* by Saeb Erekat, and the second was the novel *Memory in the Flesh* by Ahlam Mosteghanemi. He began flipping through the pages until he found the letter written between the lines of Mostaghanemi's novel in Murad's elegant handwriting, which Nur had always envied:

Dear Nur,

Sending you my warmest greetings and all my friendship. Please forgive me for writing such a short letter; I'm up to my neck in work on my study of Zionist colonialism . . . On which note, I'd like to ask you for two more books: Edward Said's *Culture and Imperialism* and Bill Ashcroft's *Postcolonial Studies*. Unrelatedly, I really wish you would stop using that revolting phrase about the bigger prison and the smaller prison . . . You don't know what the smaller one is actually like, Nur . . . It's the most horrible thing in the world. A rusty iron room . . . And as for the bigger prison, you've imprisoned yourself in it without any outside help at all. You created it . . .

* * *

Dear Nur,

I'm sorry this is rushed, but let me urge you again to drop your research on Mary Magdalene and invest your knowledge of history, archaeology, and ideology in studying contemporary issues, like the Sheikh Jarrah neighborhood in East Jerusalem, where the colonial regime is trying to evict Palestinians, or the ongoing excavations under the Al-Aqsa Mosque. Those are both pressing issues. To stand up to the colonial monster, we have to establish our own intellectual reference points.

At any rate, I won't bother you too much. Though I'd like to make one last request in closing, which is that you photograph some of the camp's main landmarks . . . I want new pictures of you, too, though I hope the next one will be of you with your arms around a beautiful girl—and that next time my mother visits, she'll announce that she's your fiancée.

Till next time, my friend . . .

He reread the letters, disappointed by Murad's harshness and brevity, then threw the novel aside irritably, lying back and glaring at the ceiling. Then he grabbed his phone again to start recording:

[MONDAY NIGHT, APRIL 19: IDEAL—MAYBE FINAL— CONCEPT FOR THE MAGDALENE NOVEL]

The ivory box has been passed down from generation to generation. It all starts with a Roman-era convert to Jesus's religion, who keeps his choice a secret at first. This believer is a follower and disciple of Magdalene; after the crucifixion, he even falls in love with her, though she doesn't know that. The follower receives the secret commandments and teachings of Jesus from the lips of Magdalene, which causes the Apostle

Peter, Jesus's rock, to protest. Magdalene fears Peter's dominance and either secrets herself away in a cave on the Mount of Olives or travels to Galilee to dwell in a cave on Mount Carmel. That's where the present-day novelist Naseem Shakr picks up, weaving a plot that imagines the discovery of a secret church devoted to Magdalene inside the cave, where manuscripts in Aramaic are found that suggest the existence of a Gospel of Mary Magdalene that includes secret teachings of Jesus. These manuscripts also reference the last wishes of Magdalene, who asked her follower to cut locks of her hair and anoint them with what remained of the nard she poured over Jesus, and to keep them in a box until the Savior returned, confirming John the Theologian's vision about Armageddon. The follower honored her wishes, and over the generations, his family passed on her secret, preserving it by assigning seven demons to watch over it throughout the Roman, Byzantine, and Muslim eras. As for the man's present-day descendants, Naseem Shakr derives his knowledge of them from the stories of the Nakba he reads as he researches the villages around the Tel Megiddo archaeological site, in addition to interviews he conducts with people displaced from those villages in 1948. He's surprised by the name of a certain shrine, uttered by an old woman displaced from the ill-fated village of Al-Lajjun, where Kibbutz Megiddo now stands: the shrine of Misk al-Attar, whose name reflects the sweet fragrance the old woman says emanates from the shrine. It's located by a well east of the village, near Tel Megiddo, and one of the miracles the righteous saint buried there used to perform was the expulsion of demons—with Mary Magdalene's aid. Note that Misk al-Attar, who is said to be buried in the depths of the well, was the last grandson of Simon the Lame.

Comment about this concept:

It's promising, and the plot can be developed and supplemented with subplots and other premises, which would require me to read up on that historical period yet again, and to resolve the issue of the narrative time. On this point, I think it's better to make the time period the present day and the genre a well-thought-out detective story—which I won't deny was inspired, in part, by Dan Brown.

PS: How I envy you your smaller prison, Murad. Your iron-barred reality has clear features and is made up of one simple but harsh equation: jail, jailed, jailer. But in this larger prison, things are less clear-cut. You want me to engage, to fight! I did fight, friend, in Jerusalem, on the heights of a Biblical summit, until I tumbled down it and landed here in this room, covered in bruises and injuries that have affected my identity and sense of being . . . But it's fine, Murad—never mind. What I'm doing now I would never put in a letter to you . . . One day, though, I will finish the Magdalene novel, and it will amaze everyone who's ever shushed me or made me feel crazy. I'm not going to send you a picture of me with the fiancée you're hoping for; instead, I'll send a picture of Magdalene and me when she enters the world as a novel.

He stopped recording, tossing his phone down beside him and turning toward the pile of books lying on the floor next to the bed. He looked through them in search of a specific book, which he found: a book about the secrets of Christian Gnosticism. He opened it to read certain paragraphs he'd already highlighted and continued reading late into the night until his eyes burned from exhaustion and he let the open book fall onto his chest, drifting off for a few moments. He awoke to the sound of gunfire reverberating through the camp's alleyways. He tossed and turned, unable to determine where it was coming from, wondering whether these were Occupation bullets or an armed spat between two groups fighting over some illusion. The shots subsided, and he went back to sleep, wrapped in his book.

CHAPTER 2

That April afternoon in Ramadan was as sweltering as summer.

And there he was, tucked into his room constructed from the shadows of the alleyways, stretched out on his bed and surrendering to the boredom creeping over him. It had been accumulating for a long time, extending and intensifying, turning into isolation. That isolation had become a cradle for a memory that lay with him night after night, giving birth to misshapen twins somewhere between past and present, camp and city, Ramallah and Jerusalem, between his father and his shadow, Nur and Or, reading and recording . . . Nur al-Shahdi lived in that in-between and flourished there, banishing its heat with Magdalene humidity.

[TUESDAY, APRIL 20, 2021: WHO IS MARY MAGDALENE?]

If I use the Misk al-Attar idea, I'll have to show the period after Jesus's crucifixion, making sure it's historically accurate and also digging deeper into all its layers—the intellectual, the religious, the cultural—to find out more about its untold stories.

These untold stories are the material for my novel, so I'll also need to do an exegetic reading of the four Synoptic Gospels, interpret the verses that reference Magdalene, and determine who the historical figure actually was, because the Gospels mention more than one Magdalene and multiple Marys. (On which point: some Western Christian literature treats all these different Marys as a single person.) The first Mary is Mary Magdalene; Jesus cast seven demons out of her, which caused her to believe in him and follow him from Galilee to Jerusalem (Luke 8:1-3). Then there's Mary the sister of Lazarus in Al-'Eizariya, or Bethany, near Jerusalem, who poured nard, a precious ointment, on Jesus's feet and dried them with her hair (John 21:3). Finally, there's yet another woman, a "sinful woman," who isn't mentioned by name, but people say she's Magdalene. According to the Gospel account, this woman was from the Galilean city of Nain, and she's the one who poured perfume on Jesus's feet, washed them with her tears, and dried them with her hair (Luke 8:37-38). Eastern Christianity keeps these women separate and sanctifies Mary Magdalene, but when we do a deep reading of their mysterious presence in the four Synoptic Gospels, Matthew, Mark, Luke, and John, we see that they are, in fact, a single woman.

It goes like this: Mary Magdalene was a wealthy tradeswoman from the town of Magdala, and she owned a luxurious house in Bethany, just outside Jerusalem. When she was possessed by seven demons, she abandoned her family and her trade to wander the wilderness and was drawn unwittingly into prostitution. Then Jesus delivered her from her demons and her life of sin, and, back in her right mind, she decided to thank him with a gift of perfume. Because she believed in and supported him, she earned his favor. A perfume that cost three hundred denarii wasn't something a simple prostitute could afford—but a wealthy woman like Magdalene could.

Magdalene represents the contradictions in life: the dual presence of good and evil, repentance and sin, angels and demons.

Meanwhile, the anointing of Jesus's feet with perfume happens twice in the Gospels: once by Mary, Lazarus's sister, and once by the sinful woman. This may suggest that it was a ritual women practiced frequently during this time period. Nor is it necessarily accurate to assume that the term "sinful woman" references a woman who engaged in adultery and prostitution . . . She might've been called a sinner in view of the traditions and customs of her religious community, and of Judaism at that time. Or maybe she was a sinner just because she believed in Jesus or because she practiced a type of secret Gnostic worship.

The fact that Jesus's first appearance after the crucifixion was to Mary Magdalene (John 20:11-18) just confirms that she was an important and influential figure, not only in Jesus's life but also in her social circles in Galilee and Jerusalem.

That said, her presence in the story is tenuous and ambiguous, like the mysterious relationship between Magdalene, Peter, and the rest of the disciples, and it needs more details, though I'll have to be careful not to overburden the narrative with it.

PS: Murad, my friend . . . I'm going to let you in on a secret now that I haven't been able to write about in our smuggled letters . . . I'll tell you about all my contradictions and nonsense. There's safety in a name, Murad, and invulnerability in a mask. And I've found a mask and a name I can use to slip into the depths of the colonial world . . . Isn't that what your buddy Frantz Fanon says about black skins and white masks?

Shapira . . . Or Shapira. Like Bond . . . James Bond. As I walk through the streets and squares of Tel Aviv and West Jerusalem, I feel like my Ashkenazi features, crowned with this name, make me a superhero in disguise, hiding his true features, like Batman, Spiderman, Superman . . . Me, I'm Or Shapira Man, but I don't feel like a superhero . . . I only feel hunted, afraid, weak, confused, and full of contradictions. All of which makes me believe for a moment in some miracle that might save me from my own helplessness . . . a miracle that would lead me to believe in some supernatural power making me, and no one else, the hero of my own dreams.

You know something?

I actually really enjoy how successful I've been in passing myself off as Or Shapira. The name is fantastic! The mask lets me be totally at ease. Using the name in our colonial reality is itself an assault on that other name that's been assaulting me since I was birthed from the alleys' womb . . . I didn't just assume the name; I also imagined it. I had the audacity to imagine . . . the audacity of someone who, in this world of loss and deprivation, has nothing to lose . . . Even my clothes are from Zionist stores and souqs, Murad . . . I would go into a store to watch "the Other" choosing his clothes and then buy the same ones . . . It's all in the details, my friend, right?

He followed up the voice memo by making his usual electronic rounds, starting with the latest news from various websites in Arabic, Hebrew, and English, all reporting the same story about escalating tensions in Jerusalem, especially around Damascus Gate and Sheikh Jarrah.

He let out a short, sharp breath as he watched the Zionist police and border guards brutalize the residents of Sheikh Jarrah and the demonstrators standing with them, then clicked away from the news to check the websites of his favorite archaeological and historical institutes. Nothing new on the Arabic sites, so he moved on to Hebrew, where he found news that excavation work was nearing completion at a Byzantine dig site, the largest in the Middle East, near the depopulated village of Yibna in southern Palestine. Then he moved to the English sites and paused on the page for the W.F. Albright Institute of Archaeological Research, which was announcing its second dig season for the Roman Sixth Legion camp near Megiddo. He finished his electronic browsing by checking his emails and call log, looking for a sign or at least a missed call from Sheikh Morsi, but there was nothing. Radio silence.

He'd been waiting, expectant, for a month and a half. Sheikh

Morsi had told him, "Go back to Ramallah for now . . . It's too dangerous for you to stay in Jerusalem."

So here he was in this room, a capsized ship, and he and his whole being had been dumped into the raging, rolling sea of memory as he searched for some safe harbor, for Jerusalem to return to how she was when he first arrived in the spring of 2016, when she offered him newer and better circumstances. That was when he landed his job as a tour guide for pilgrims and tourists from all over the world who came to visit Jerusalem and her environs. The long-suffering Nur had just graduated from the Institute of Archaeology, and one of his professors, impressed by his student's passion and his excellence in history and archaeology, advised him to start off by working freelance in archaeology and tourism to make a name for himself. It would help him gain experience and knowledge that could act as a base for his continued education later on. In the end, his professor Bahjat Najwan helped him sort out his work situation, too, taking advantage of his close relationship with Shakib al-Qassabi, the owner of one of the biggest travel agencies in Jerusalem, to enumerate Nur's talents and merits in the field, the most important of which were his mastery of Hebrew and English and his vast subject area expertise, especially with regard to Palestine in the Roman and Byzantine periods. Nur's good looks didn't hurt, either. It was his appearance that prompted Shakib al-Qassabi to reluctantly overlook his refugee origins and his occasionally slipping into Jerusalem without a work permit, though he made sure to inform his friend Bahjat that he would deny any connection to Nur if the tourist police or border guards detained him with a false ID.

Then, in Jerusalem, Morsi al-Gharnati appeared. Sheikh Morsi, as he liked to be called, was a guardian and shepherd for Nur, the stranger emerging from the depths of the alleyways.

Sheikh Morsi came from the Silsila neighborhood in the Old City and was around forty, a tall man with a charming dark complexion and North African roots, redolent of Sufism and Andalusia. He was drawn to Nur's quiet brevity and welcoming silence.

With a few self-assured words, Nur captured his interest, reinforcing it with his calm, uncomplaining obedience and his tendency not to interfere in things that didn't concern him. Sheikh Morsi embraced him wholeheartedly, using his own standing with Shakib al-Qassabi to Nur's advantage. Shakib wasn't sure Nur would be able to keep working for him; beginnings are always difficult, especially for a young Palestinian refugee sneaking into Jerusalem to work without a permit. But Sheikh Morsi, who'd been working for Shakib since he was fifteen, just like his father, Rukn al-Din al-Gharnati, before him, instructed Nur in the basics of the profession with patience and composure, lavishing him with his knowledge and experience and revealing to him, in the process, a different Jerusalem than the one he'd read about in books and online: to Nur, Sheikh Morsi's Jerusalem was infinitely more glorious.

Nur did not disappoint; he amazed Sheikh Morsi with his quickness to learn, his eloquence, and the breadth of his knowledge, and he moved up the ranks rapidly, becoming a fullfledged tour guide, accompanying foreign delegations and tour groups not only in the alleyways of Jerusalem's Old City but also in Bethlehem and Nazareth, especially during the Christian holidays. That was the atmosphere in which Mary Magdalene emerged from the pages of Dan Brown's *Da Vinci Code* and lodged inside him at the height of his immersion in the tourism profession, one of the biggest perks of which was his exposure to the latest information on archaeological discoveries and historical research.

He realized, deep down, that he immersed himself in this work to flee emptiness and abandonment, disappointment, silence, desolation and uncertainty, and that he was distancing himself from the shadows. The shadows of a father indifferent to his son's studies and work. And so Nur rejected the alleyways, his father's disappointment, and the quivering, ephemeral atmosphere of Ramallah.

That alienating immersion, coupled with a certain boldness Nur had picked up at the flea market in Jaffa and the new language on his tongue, pronounced with Ashkenazi eloquence, led him to participate in seminars and conferences held in Jerusalem, Haifa, and Tel Aviv for global leaders in archaeology and research. As for his ticket to that other world garnished with colonialism and sprinkled with modernity and culture, fraught with risk and the possibility of being caught red-handed with a persona that wasn't his, it was thanks to Or Shapira's ID card. When he disclosed the secret of that identity, it was a disclosure that, like all of Nur's secrets, came with traditions and rules, the most important of which was softening his usual silence in exchange for a slight increase in what he allowed himself to share with a specific person who made him feel safe. That person was Sheikh Morsi, to whom Nur entrusted Or Shapira's ID card two years after he found it, asking him for help in forging it, replacing Or's picture with his own. Nur was certain that Sheikh Morsi, a son of Jerusalem and its hidden depths and secret places, was the only one capable of helping.

That evening, Sheikh Morsi had warned him. "Are you sure you want to take the risk?"

"Yes."

"And you know that getting caught with a fake ID is different from being caught without a work permit? The consequences are dire . . . "

"I know that, too."

"*And* you know that the Shapira family is one of the oldest Ashkenazi families around?"

"I do."

Sheikh Morsi was glad to help. He was reassured by his

confidence in Nur, as well as Nur's confidence in himself and the way the young man avoided nonsense like gossip, meddling, and showing off. A week later, he was back, holding Nur's new mask.

As soon as Nur took the card into his own hands to examine it, scrutinizing his flawless Ashkenazi image, he felt something painful and mysterious. Something was gnawing at him. The mask was no longer just about his features but had extended to permeate his identity and blur it with someone else's. He frowned. *Am I really doing this? Impersonating an Ashkenazi Zionist? What if he finds out? What if he catches me in the act, wearing his shadow and carrying his ID on some stupid street in Jerusalem or Tel Aviv?*

Then I'll take him by surprise—I'll attack first. I'll say, "Who are you? You're not Or. I'm Or Shapira."

"No, I'm Or Shapira; you stole my identity! Who are you? Tell me!"

"Like I said, I'm Or."

"Then what's your father's name?"

"Nitzan."

"Your mother's name?"

"Lital."

"Your grandfather's name?"

Silence.

"Your grandmother's name?"

Silence.

"See?! You idiot! You're not me—so who are you?"

"I am you . . . I'm your mirror image."

In his Ashkenazi mask-wearing quest, Nur only rarely dared to actually wear the mask and use the counterfeit ID; typically, he just used the name. As for his identity, his features and fluency in Hebrew were enough to ensure his safe passage to the historical, archaeological destinations he favored in his search for the origins and fate of Mary Magdalene. Nur no longer lived on the edges but in the depths of the center, the center of the Otherness he'd constructed from the alleyways of the Nakba.

He realized as much as he plunged into Or Shapira's identity; he'd been on the verge of falling into a bottomless abyss of uncertainty, only for his friend Murad, from the gloom of his cell, to inadvertently pull him back, unaware as he was of the siren call of Nur's blue-and-white mask. He pulled him back with books and studies chock full of the origins, parameters, and history of colonialism and the emergence of Zionism, its goals, and the roots of its political and geographic reality, leaving Nur gasping, inhaling refugee air as he returned to himself: displaced, misshapen, ill-fated. Nur al-Shahdi didn't back away from Or Shapira's identity but instead confronted it. Now, when he wore it, he was fully aware of where it came from, and this awareness granted him immunity, keeping him from becoming yet another black skin/white mask situation, like the people Murad's Frantz Fanon wrote about.

At least until the day when Nur shouted out all the names he'd learned, the day that caused the month and a half of isolation he was still enduring.

That day, Shakib al-Qassabi had assigned him to guide an American tour group to the forested area of Sar'a, west of Jerusalem. At the time, Nur objected, though only on the inside; his contract with the company was to receive and accompany tourist groups to the Old City, to show them its religious and historical landmarks, and he was an experienced group leader on the Via Dolorosa, the fourteen stops of Jesus before his crucifixion on Mount Calvary, where the Church of the Holy Sepulchre now stood. However, the decline in tourism due to the coronavirus pandemic and his need for a salary and the tips tourists showered on him prompted him to agree, if reluctantly. Only Sheikh Morsi felt his discomfort and aversion to accompanying the group to Sar'a, so he walked with him to the minibus door and whispered to him, "Hang in there, Nur. Work is work. All you have to do is talk."

Nur mumbled something and nodded, relenting, then greeted the bus in his remarkably good English and carried on as usual all the way to the Tzora Forest, as it was called, pointing out the window at noteworthy archaeological and religious sites and bolstering that information with details about historical events that took place nearby. Finally, after half an hour, the bus turned onto a narrow side road that led to a hill crowned by a historic landmark and surrounded by forested slopes overlooking the western outskirts of Jerusalem. The bus stopped beside a winding path leading to a Biblical site whose horrors and secrets Nur had learned by heart from publications put out by the Zionist Ministry of Tourism; it was the site of the Biblical village of Zorah, or Sar'a, the birthplace of the Old Testament superhero Samson the Mighty.

The tourists got off the bus and followed Nur along the narrow path that cut through the greenery, lined with shaded wooden benches where they could rest, and listened with enjoyment to Nur's rousing recitation of touristic details as he gestured animatedly, his voice robotic, at a firm remove from his real identity and refugee origins: "We are now walking in the footsteps of Samson, through a forest dedicated to the memory of Chaim Weizmann, the first president of the state of Israel.

"The story of this Old Testament site and its transformation into an enchanting tourist destination began in 1991 when the Israel Land Fund decided to extend invitations to over thirty-seven artists and sculptors, most of whom were new immigrants from Russia and Eastern Europe. The fund's management offered them huge pieces of rock from the area so they could carve statues and artistic masterpieces inspired by the events and stories in the Torah, especially the story of Samson and Delilah . . . Thus, this deserted path was transformed into the trail of sculptures you can now see on both sides, leading to the tomb of Samson and his father, Manoah, at the top of the hill . . ."

They climbed the hill and reached the shrine, constructed of stone with two small white domes atop it. On the wall of the shrine was a sign in Hebrew that read, "The Tomb of the Hero Samson and His Father Manoah." Next to the shrine was a seating area with wide wooden benches overlooking the western hills of Jerusalem and her forests, in addition to Deir Rafat, the lofty Catholic monastery guarded by the giant statue of the Virgin Mary adorning its façade.

Then, mid-spiel, Nur stopped talking, choking on his words about the Torah and on the lump burning his throat. Some of the tourists thought he was out of breath from climbing the hill and speaking with such animation, and an elderly lady from his group approached him sympathetically to offer him a sip of water from her bottle. He looked at her in silence for a few moments, gasping for air, then looked around anxiously, as if searching for something he'd lost a long time ago. Then, all at once, he climbed the low wall of the shrine, scrambled onto the roof, and began to speak again, giving an impassioned and electrifying address that he delivered in a wounded screech.

"Actually, ladies and gentlemen, no . . . You believe in the coming salvation; let me appeal to your pure ears, innocent hearts, and devout consciences and tell you that everything I just said is complete nonsense. Pure, baseless fantasy. On this spot where you're standing, ladies and gentlemen, once lay the rubble of the Palestinian Arab village of Sar'a. It was destroyed, and its four hundred inhabitants were displaced, during the Nakba in July 1948 . . . Yes, displaced. Now they've been crammed into refugee camps. Zionist militias destroyed the village to build Kibbutz Tzora in its place. Right now, you're standing on the house of the village leader, and the shrine I'm standing on is none other than the shrine of Sheikh Samit. The people of this village and neighboring villages used to seek his blessing, offering him vows and sacrifices in hopes that he would help them conceive and have children. That's right, ladies and gentlemen, there's no Samson here to mourn, no superhero. Superheroes don't have graves. Samson is like Superman; he never dies.

"And as for this spot, where you're standing, there was nothing but catastrophe—Nakba—and a people displaced from their land."

Then Nur fell silent, his throat closing again, and jumped down from the shrine's roof amidst the gasps and uneasy glances of the American tourists, walking quickly away from them as he descended the hill, away from the madness of history, Nakba, and displacement, leaving the crowd open-mouthed in his wake, stricken by the sharpness of his tone and his talk of catastrophe, his sudden frenzy. When Shakib al-Qassabi, the head of the tour company, found out about his speech on the Nakba, Nur was forced to give up his only source of livelihood, as well. Al-Qassabi fired him in an outpouring of fury and indignation, and Sheikh Morsi patted him on the shoulder with a chuckle, gently suggesting that he disappear into the darkest alleyways of his camp so the Zionist Ministry of Tourism wouldn't discover his secret. So Nur hid, concealing himself in his room, where, at last, he was reborn from the womb of Mary Magdalene.

* * *

In the afternoon, which showed no sign of a breeze, he felt suddenly overwhelmed by his smell and the sticky sweat covering his body, so he made his way to the shower to rinse off the oppressive heat and regain some energy and clarity. The minutes felt heavy, but time wasn't creeping over Nur; instead, Nur crept along beneath it. Slowly.

Time was dense and alluring, feverishly lazy, ravenous for monotony, boredom, irritability, and disgust. A dazed, disgusted

Nur moaned in the shower, whiling away the minutes of his futile day. The house around him was still. His father was trying to beat the fast by sleeping so as to escape the heat, thirst, and his craving for a cigarette. Nur couldn't tell whether Khadija was asleep, but she deferred to his father's idleness.

Refreshed after his shower, he directed his steps toward the kitchen and opened the fridge, not craving anything particular, just nourishment; a memory as predatory as his could be sated only with something fatty, fuel its monstrous sense of time would use to devour him.

Then he climbed the stairs to his room, tempted by the clarity of his mind and the silence surrounding him to record a new voice memo.

[TUESDAY AFTERNOON, APRIL 20, 2021:
MARY MAGDALENE'S PERFUME]

Mary therefore took a pound of expensive ointment made from pure nard, and anointed the feet of Jesus and wiped his feet with her hair. The house was filled with the fragrance of the perfume. (John 12:3)[1]

And behold, a woman of the city, who was a sinner, when she learned that he was reclining at table in the Pharisee's house, brought an alabaster flask of ointment, and standing behind him at his feet, weeping, she began to wet his feet with her tears and wiped them with the hair of her head and kissed his feet and anointed them with the ointment. (Luke 7:37-38)

This scene is so lovely! It's captivating, and described so

---

[1] English Standard Version. All Biblical citations are taken from this translation.

precisely that all it's missing is a soundtrack of tears and sighs . . . What a scene of holy passion! But I don't understand—why didn't the authors discuss the jealousy and resentment of some of the other disciples?

Judas Iscariot wasn't the only one who denounced Magdalene's action; there were others, too, who denounced it, not because of a general aversion to wastefulness but because it had won Magdalene Jesus's favor and affection . . . Which brings me to my non-Synoptic sources, the ones that were silenced and excluded from the sacred text. These are the Gnostic gospels, which shed light on Magdalene's presence in Jesus's life and her pivotal role in it after entering his inner circle . . . This is what we find in the Gospel of Philip, which Dan Brown refers to in that revolting novel of his. But before talking about that gospel, in the final text of my novel, I have to mention how the Gnostic gospels were found in the Egyptian village of Nag Hammadi on the banks of the Nile, north of Luxor. A complete Gnostic library was discovered by chance there in 1945, and its contents were published in 1980. There were fifty-two gospels hidden there, in a large clay jar . . . Among them were parts of the Gospel of Mary Magdalene, in addition to the Gospels of Philip and Thomas and a lot of Gnostic letters and documents.

PS: You know something, Murad? At first, my discovery that I looked kind of Ashkenazi was just a diversion. An adventure. And then you surprised me with the letters you had smuggled out of detention, and the thought-provoking books, and I realized that, in a world that has concealed and distorted my original features, this is what I have left. These features are my identity . . . That's how I came up with my alter ego. At first, I borrowed different names as I got into the details of what you call Zionist colonialism; sometimes my name was Nati, sometimes Rafi or Benjamin. And then I stumbled across the best one in the pocket of that leather jacket: Shapira . . . Or Shapira

. . . and the name stuck with me like the Joker. Incidentally, have you seen the *Joker* movie with Joaquin Phoenix?

This name is my ace in the hole that I can play in the most difficult situations, and it's my backup plan when things get complicated. It has followed me like my shadow until all at once I felt—because of you—that I'd sold my real shadow for a fake ID and become shadowless. I was voiceless in my father's shadow, and now I'm shadowless *and* voiceless because I've dressed myself up in a new identity, complete with the Star of David I used to wear to history seminars at Bar Ilan University in Tel Aviv, or the Hebrew University, or one of Jerusalem's research centers.

This identity seemed to have a seductive force that pushed me to merge with it and hold on tightly. I felt it cling to me . . . to my long, curly hair, my blue eyes, and my Ashkenazi-accented Hebrew with its heavy *r*'s, its *Ha* sound that becomes a *kha*, and its letter *'ayn* that morphs into a silent hamza, a glottal stop. I'm constantly amazed by how important features and faces are in the Zionist public square. They're pre-determined categories in Tel Aviv, but it's not like that everywhere . . . My features are as indigenous as anyone else's among my occupied people, but I've gamed the system using the value colonial standards assign them. That value gets its meaning from racism, divine right, perception, and prejudice; my charming face won't give me an edge in New York, Paris, or London unless I'm seducing a beautiful woman. Here, though, it gives me that edge, and it gives generously.

He ended the recording feeling emotional and missing Murad tremendously, and looked around his room, inspecting it carefully, inspecting his notebooks and junk, archaeological memorabilia, books and scattered papers, the wardrobe, his leather jacket. Then he grabbed his phone and went back to the Albright Institute's website, poring over the details of the news he had read just a few hours prior:

The W.F. Albright Institute of Archaeological Research, in cooperation with the Israel Antiquities Authority, is pleased to announce the opening of the second excavation season for the Jezreel Valley Regional Project south of Tel Megiddo under the title, "The Roman Sixth Legion: Between Reality and Myth."

The institute's administration is also pleased to welcome interested researchers or volunteers in the field of archaeology to join the expedition, which will be headquartered at the Kibbutz Mishmar HaEmek for one month, from April 26 to May 26, 2021.

For more details, please visit the institute's Jerusalem address at 26 Salah ed-Din Street.

Please note: The registration deadline for those wishing to join the expedition is at 3 P.M. on Thursday, April 22, 2021.

He pondered the invitation. He'd been following the Albright Institute's activities for a while now. Several months prior, he'd attended a lecture there on the historical fortress of Masada, given by a distinguished American professor in the fields of history and archaeology. Nur was well aware that the institute was one of the oldest American research centers for ancient Near Eastern studies. It was established in 1900 as the American School of Oriental Research and was renamed in 1970 in honor of the famous American Biblical archaeologist, William Albright, for his role in discovering and identifying the Dead Sea Scrolls, which had been found in the caves of Wadi Qumran, south of Jericho, in the early twentieth century.

He threw his phone down beside him in irritation and surrendered to the bitter reality of his isolation and the time he was smashing into pieces; he gathered up moments and scattered them in vain in the early evening light of his room. He didn't have the slightest desire to break free from the silence of the house to roam the streets of Ramallah and interrupt the heavy rhythm of time; he hadn't left his room since his forced return from Jerusalem, except for yesterday, to meet Umm Adli.

Because where would Nur go?

Time had no meaning for him in this camp; he had no memories in Ramallah, no groans or moans or rumpling of bedsheets, no love or longing. Nothing here but his voice memos, recording and listening to them, and the seduction of his secret habit and the tremors it sent through his body, here in this room perched atop a small house built from the alleys: the alleys of the camp in Ramallah, Ramallah in chaos and the daily sins and blunders that led Nur into silence. Here in Ramallah there were no masks, just as there were no features.

Here Nur was less than human but more than a mere creature, his identity pounced upon, chased, hunted down, and devoured. There was no life in Ramallah because life was a negotiation, and negotiations needed a street, and he was the street, the slave paved over with everything his father had reduced to remnants . . . to shreds. To alleyways of silence and murmurs.

But where was he headed? What was his destination?

How had his circumstances and his fate turned so upside down, alienating him so fully from his alleyway reality and pulling him away from his initial misshapenness to don a mask he'd crafted from his own features, now the features of the Other. There, in Jerusalem and Tel Aviv, was Nur Nur or was he his Other, Or?

No . . . No masks in Ramallah. Ramallah itself was the mask.

In the splendor of isolation seasoned with true silence, Nur al-Shahdi realized more than ever that he'd been living in the shadows of masks for thirty years. He wore the mask of his own features and of Or Shapira. His father's mask was silence, and the camp's mask was all of Ramallah. A mask needs time, and time doesn't do it the favor of skipping ahead. No, it's immersed, surrounded in time, enveloped by the smells of cement, rust, humidity, moss, mold, fear, and pursuit.

It was Nur, now, who grappled with the features and ways of life of the alleyways and this cursed house. He'd been born from the death of his mother, who died only once, and he lived in the shadow of a silent father who'd decided to die in stages. How many times had his father died in front of him—how many?

Their disordered relationship was haunted by fates that weren't his; it was a relationship in which Nur had felt the presence of his father only once, when he was ten years old and a student at the camp's elementary school, where the taunting and bullying had wrecked him. That day, Nur came home from school in tears. He went to his room and took out a big pair of scissors, cutting off his long, honey-coloured curls, convinced that no one in the house would even notice. Khadija was a parched land searching for rain to quench her thirst, his father Mahdi a cloudless desert sky. But it was a rare day of paternal feeling. Mahdi spotted him and leapt up, shaken, abandoning his silence and his favorite living room sofa to rush toward his only son. He clutched his head in his hands and cried out in his gruff voice, "Who did this to you?"

"Me."

"Why?"

"Because I'm a boy, not a girl. I'm not Nura."

"Who called you Nura?"

"The kids at school."

Mahdi went crazy. He didn't sleep a wink that night, his body burning with cigarettes and curses, and as soon as the morning came, he accompanied Nur to school for the first time in his life, astonishing some of the camp's residents by running there with Nur's hand in his, poor Nur whose short legs lagged behind as he stared up at his father in disbelief that he was holding his hand. They made it to school just as the students were getting ready to line up for morning assembly in the main courtyard. Mahdi and Nur pushed through the crowds of students until they reached the platform where the bewildered teachers stood with the school principal, whom Mahdi pulled violently toward him by the collar, saying in a loud, stern voice, the kind Nur craved from him, "If Nur ever comes home and cuts off all his hair again, I'll cut off your mustache—get it?"

The principal, drowning in Mahdi's threats and warnings amidst the chaos of the schoolyard, didn't respond. So Mahdi turned on his heels and stalked away, leaving behind his son, who was swelling with pride. That was his father, his Baba. That day, he not only had a few moments with the father who'd been lost to him, but he also found a friend in Murad, and a protector.

Now what was he doing?

He was fed up with this tango, tired of the equivocation; now he wished that his memory was stored on his cell phone so that he could easily delete it, throw it into the virtual trash can. How easy technology was! It didn't carry any hidden resentments, but it had a remarkable ability to forget with the touch of a button.

He grabbed his phone reflexively and went back to the Albright Institute's invitation, which he examined closely; then he jumped out of bed and paced his room, the field of his imagination. How vast it was now, how wide! So much space!

Then he came back down from the heights to the miserable reality of the room, to the house, the alleyway, the camp, Ramallah, the country, the sky, questioning his reality as soon as he'd formulated it: *Who am I? Who is my father? What are the alleyways? Where is my identity? Where's my shadow? And my mirror? What am I doing here?*

There were no special developments for him here, no events, no incidents or occasions, no ingredients for a new memory, no holidays or new clothes, no life to mourn, no friendship, no love, no poetry or dancing . . .

He'd abandoned the camp a long time ago, ever since his father got out of detention, since Murad was arrested. As for

Ramallah, he'd never mastered it. He'd never felt it. There were two types of cities: the kind with a womb and the kind without. Natural birth vs. artificial insemination. Stones and fragrance vs. iron and rust. Jerusalem vs. Ramallah, and he had embraced Jerusalem, freed from the burdens of Ramallah.

Nur was seeking freedom; he didn't want to die in stages like his father. His father had been expiring in silence ever since Noura and her curls passed away, since his exile in prison, since his homeland betrayed him and he was deprived of seeing his son. Ever since his muddled mind and madness, and his muteness. Only someone who is dying in stages can feel that emptiness that expands, lodging little by little on the left side of the chest, within the heart. The heart that turns into a black hole ready to swallow up its owner. And his father was at the bitter end, about to disappear into that hole. But Nur didn't want that kind of emptiness. Nur would give birth to his own father and mother. He would give birth to his own identity, return to himself, burn his mask . . . and rise from its ashes. He would pull himself back from his contemplation and obsessions.

The Maghrib call to prayer sounded. It was time for iftar, time to break the fast, time for people to breathe a sigh of relief after a hot day. He made up his mind and got dressed quickly, taking advantage of the empty streets and alleyways to go visit the graves of his mother and grandmother in the Al-Bireh cemetery. He slipped out of the house without causing the slightest disturbance or commotion that might attract the attention of his father and Khadija. He walked through the alleyways, jogged, ran as eagerly as though he were meeting his mother for a tasty Ramadan iftar. He entered the cemetery, plunging past the tombstones, and finally reached the two graves, which stood at the north end of the plot, shaded by the cypress he'd planted fifteen years before. He stood there for a moment, his chest heaving as he caught his breath, contemplating the two graves: Sumayyah's and Noura's. Death had no mask. Death was death. He went up to his mother's grave and put his hand on the headstone. *Now what?* The night felt lifeless. Was he supposed to spread his palms and recite Sura al-Fatiha? Talk to her? Wail and gnash his teeth? No—he needed to humble himself; any confessions he made should spring organically from the stillness of the cemetery.

Whole vistas of revelation opened up to the rhythm of the wail he intoned on his mother's tomb, the headstone a harp of longing that transformed the night into dawn as he wept uncontrollably, embracing both the headstone and his torment, yearning for a mother he'd never known and had glimpsed only in the rare photograph and the few mementos he'd gathered from his grandmother, Sumayyah. Then he sat back against the gravestone. His tears subsided, and he pulled his phone from his pocket, clearing his throat before he pressed the record button:

[Evening, April 20: Thoughts About Magdalene
at My Mother's Grave]

It's dawn . . . love leads her to him, enveloped in a cloud of perfume. It's the same perfume that emanates from him. From his distant corner, it leads her. Guides her. It's dawn . . . Magdalene treads on her heartache. She wavers, weeps. And in the dim glow of morning, a grave without a stone . . . No one's inside. She keels over, leaning into the divine promise, and weeps . . . a wounded moan that dies away when she catches a glimpse of the light surrounding her. She's startled and turns toward its source, and there is her beloved, in all his promise and light, standing upright, approaching her. He bends over her. Takes a lock of her hair . . . wipes her tears with it. She asks in a whisper, "Is it you? Is it you, my soul? My self?"

PS: I'm not going to miss out on this opportunity with the Albright Institute . . . The invitation's a sign from Magdalene.

Her blessing for me to go to the very cradle of the novel, where it all begins. It's time for me to engage. It's time for me to reclaim myself. I'll wear the Or Shapira mask for the last time. It'll be my last dance. My last dance, Murad . . . I swear it on my mother's soul . . .

He put the phone back in his pocket. For more than half an hour, he sat staring into the void without a whisper, then stood abruptly. What was Nur thinking?

He set out for home. There was some modest activity outside now, suggesting that the streets and alleyways would soon be packed with people as they finished iftar. He quickened his steps, feeling dozens of eyes following and surveilling him as he walked without a mask; he felt naked and broke into a run. Arriving home, he climbed the stairs to his room, quickly closed the door behind him as he tried to catch his breath, and sat down on the edge of the bed. Then he lay back and stared at the ceiling . . . What was he doing? What was he going to do? Did he suddenly have the supernatural power to put an end to his time of isolation in the alleys?

He contemplated the room, his eyes settling on his Ashkenazi leather jacket, and then he leapt out of bed, hurried to his closet, and pulled out a small wooden box. From it, he took a blue ID card and a gold Star of David necklace. He put these in his trousers pocket, then took out the money he had left and counted it: $1,200, which he divided in half—$600 for him, $600 for his father and Khadija. He grabbed a large backpack lying next to the closet, stuffing whatever clothes he could find into it, as well as some folders containing research for his novel. Then he made one last sweep through the room, the last dance before leaving it and his isolation behind, a knife at the throat of alley time. He was intoxicated by the freedom. He paused in the living room, where he caught sight of the back of Khadija's head as she sat immersed in a Ramadan TV series. His father wasn't home. His father was with the cart, and the cart was with his father. Coffee, tea, and sahlab . . .

He placed the money on the wooden table, then headed toward the door. The escape hatch from the horrors of silence and the hell of a father who was on the brink of dying from disappointment and betrayal. He stood there for a moment without turning around, afraid of turning toward memory, then opened the door and made a call to someone he knew well, speaking firmly: "Sheikh Morsi, I'm on my way to you. To Jerusalem . . ."

Part II

Or

Jesus said, "Blessings on the lion that the human will eat, so that the lion becomes human. And cursed is the human that the lion will eat, and the lion will become human."
—The Gospel of Thomas, Logion 7[2]

[2] *The Gnostic Gospels of Jesus: The Definitive Collection of Mystical Gospels and Secret Books About Jesus of Nazareth*, edited and translated by Marvin Meyer (HarperCollins, 2005). All citations from the Gnostic texts are taken from this translation, except where otherwise noted.

CHAPTER 3

Hello, my name is Or . . . Or Shapira."

He stared again at his reflection in the mirror. He cleared his throat and said, with the utmost Hebrew seriousness, "Good day. I'm Or . . . Or Shapira."

He turned away, then faced the mirror and paused, forcing a fake smile that exuded charm: "Of course, I've been an amateur archaeologist since I was a kid . . . I work as a tour guide now, too."

He wrinkled his nose and grumbled, "Too braggy. I doubt Or would introduce himself like that . . . "

He headed toward the window of the east-facing room, opening it to take in a scene that had always captivated him: the Dome of the Rock Mosque, the afternoon sun glinting in rhapsodies off its gilded dome, lending it the ambrosial splendor of a bride. Breathtaking.

The dome was the bridal veil of Jerusalem and her mosque, adrift in lapis lazuli and turquoise, and the rock inside was her heart, beating with holiness and the blood of the earth and sky together. Someone once said that for anyone who died near the rock, it would be as if they'd died in heaven . . . who was that?

He contemplated it, the sanctuary of the Al-Aqsa Mosque . . . The courtyard was the scarf draped around the rock, and the city's thobe was embroidered with the minarets of her mosques, the towers of her churches and monasteries, her domes and arches, and her ancient homes; as for the wall, it was a sash, safeguarding her. Jerusalem was a woman, created from blood, sky, Isra' and Mi'raj, prophets and angels, demons and evil spirits, wars, horrors, blessings, and curses. She was a woman who'd been besieged throughout her various twists of fate more than thirty times, and she kept rebuilding her houses from the ruins—like this one, in the mirrors of whose ancient rooms Nur al-Shahdi was reflected back as Or Shapira. It was a house in whose timeworn rooms, if he examined them, he would feel all her old names, from Jebus to Bait al-Maqdis, or the Holy House. Names repeated by all who passed through her and scratched her body with their swords, spears, rifles, and cannons. For Jerusalem builds her glory from her ruins: sometimes a heavenly glory, sometimes an earthly one.

Nur courted her, danced with her, loved her before and still, lived in one of her rooms in a house built from the alleyways and arches of the Silsila neighborhood west of Al-Aqsa, in the middle of the Old City. Silsila was the belt at the waist of glorious Jerusalem.

This was the Jerusalem whose intent Nur had always wondered about: if this land were truly holy, why was she so savagely thirsty for blood?

Looking across at the dome, he felt the need to record a new voice memo, to organize his thoughts about the novel. He sat down on the edge of the warm bed, feeling enveloped by antiquity, like a fragrance. This little room, at least, remained untouched by the alleyways, by orphanhood, rust, and darkness.

[WEDNESDAY AFTERNOON, APRIL 21 – JERUSALEM:
MAGDALENE AND PETER]

We can get at the Gnostic worldview by answering several questions. Who are we? Where are we going? What is the light? How is it we're born from the light? And why does the Gnostic see himself as a stranger to this world?

What I have in mind with respect to Gnosticism is to conduct a critical study of the relationship between Peter and Magdalene, traced through the Gnostic schools that were widespread during the first two centuries after the crucifixion. One of the most important texts that reveals the nature of their relationship is a Gnostic Christian text called *Pistis Sophia*, passed along to us and translated by Firas al-Sawwah in his book *The Gospel's Riddles*. In one scene, Peter complains about Mary monopolizing the conversation with Jesus when he's the one with seniority and asks Jesus to silence her, but Jesus rebukes him. After that, Mary tells Jesus she can't speak freely with him for fear of Peter, who hates women, and Jesus tells her, "Whoever the Spirit inspires has the right to speak, whether man or woman."

The text paints a clear picture of Magdalene and Peter's relationship and has important implications for the novel; it will help me pin down a baseline reference for the plot so I can emphasize Peter's motives for renouncing Magdalene. It will also help me depict—with the power of imagination!—Magdalene fleeing with her followers out of fear of persecution from Peter and hiding away, either on the Mount of Olives or on Galilee's Mount Carmel, awaiting the right time to record the secret doctrines of Jesus.

PS: Murad, my friend, talking to you in these voice memos is such a relief, even though I know you'll never hear them. You're somehow both present and absent, alive and dead . . . Didn't you once call prison the cemetery of the living? Anyway, I'm in the heart of Jerusalem now . . . Can you believe it?

I arrived a little bit before dawn yesterday, stealing in like a lover through one of the gaps in the apartheid wall between the Jerusalem suburbs and the Arab village of Al-Ramm. Is it really an apartheid wall, Murad, or is it more of a threshold between two contradictory worlds: that of the center and that of the margins? The world of Or Shapira and the world of Nur al-Shahdi?

The irony is that when I sneak into Jerusalem, I do it without a mask . . . I sneak in as Nur al-Shahdi, the young Palestinian refugee . . . But when I roam her streets, I'm none other than Or Shapira . . . Now, I feel like you're going to get all up in arms and say, "Don't you have any other options, Nur? Are you really going to imitate a Zionist for the sake of a novel? What the hell?"

No, rest assured, I'm still Nur; I'm just him on the inside. Or is the outside shell. I'm the inward self, the hidden; he's the manifest exterior. I'm the interior self, the hidden; he's the manifest exterior. When the interior reveals itself, the manifest is concealed.

In any case, I wanted to tell you that my silence is dying away here . . . It's become light and swift, soaring. When I disentangled myself from the burden of my father's silence, I didn't carry my memory with me. All I brought was my mask and my novel project for a last dance, which will not be a tango . . . My final resting place won't be my memories, either, but the Magdalene novel. Mary Magdalene, who led me back here, despite the risks and challenges.

Don't get all derisive like you usually do and tell me how weirdly lucky I am that there's an old military camp being excavated so close to the destroyed village of Al-Lajjun, beside historical Tel Megiddo. It's not luck; it's a sign of Magdalene's blessing, and I'm welcoming it with all my heart, along with my mask, which I'll use to sneak into the untouched land of my novel, where Misk al-Attar lives. The land I'll grant to my main character, Naseem Shakr, for him to write the events of his novel. My novel . . . But yes, Murad, this will be the last time . . .

His voice memo was interrupted by a faint knock on the door, followed by the entrance of Sheikh Morsi, tall and dark, crowned with a green skullcap and clad in a white jalabiya, which he wore only during the month of Ramadan. He was carrying a plate of food: sesame-covered Jerusalem ka'ak bread, olive oil with local za'atar, boiled eggs, and labaneh. He placed the food on the wooden table and said, with his usual cheerfulness, "Zainab says you've been awake since noon but turned down her invitation to eat . . . Come on, you need food."

Nur hung his head, flushed with shame; it was Ramadan, and he hadn't fasted for years. Quietly, embarrassed, he said, "Please excuse me, Sheikh; I won't have even a bite until it's time to break the fast with you."

"No, you'll eat now . . . Dig in!"

It was Sheikh Morsi's habit to overlook Nur's failure to adhere to his religious duties, and he didn't insist that he fast in his home. This was why Sheikh Morsi's Sufism appealed to Nur; the man breathed out tolerance and faith, believing in a way that didn't harm anyone.

Nur scolded him. "How can you bring me food and encourage me to violate the Holy Month in your own home?"

"God forbid I urge you to commit a sin. But God Almighty didn't create us already devout and observant. We were created lacking, so we could spend our journey through life making up for our shortcomings."

"Am I lacking, Sheikh?"

Sheikh Morsi grinned and pulled him into a playful headlock. "You're lacking food, and anybody lacking food is lacking brainpower, too. Come on . . . eat!"

Nur had no sooner begun to swallow a bite of ka'ak dipped in oil and za'atar than Sheikh Morsi pulled out a paper folder and tossed it down next to him, saying, "I brought you your CV in English, too—as requested, Mr. Or Shapira."

Nur stopped eating and pounced eagerly on the folder to inspect it. The previous night had seen a tumultuous late evening meeting between the two of them. He'd asked Sheikh Morsi for some papers proving his employment in Shakib Al-Qassabi's company—but with a final request: that the papers be under Or Shapira's name rather than his own. Sheikh Morsi, who had received Nur warmly and been a generous host, had snapped: "That's pushing it, Nur . . . It's really too much. Why are you doing this? You're so determined to land yourself in trouble—and in prison. Why??"

"I'm not, Sheikh Morsi; of course I'm not . . . This is the last time I'll ask you for anything. But joining this expedition is the best thing I could do to finish my novel . . . "

"What novel, Nur? What kind of novel requires you to risk your life? Are you really that enamored of Mary Magdalene?"

"That much and more, Sheikh . . . But it's fine. I won't ask more of you than you can handle. I'll go now . . . "

"Where will you go, you idiot? Jerusalem's burning! Didn't you notice the state of the streets? It's a war zone out there . . . Things are bad right now, Nur, and Jerusalem has turned into an army outpost."

"Don't worry about it; I can handle myself . . . Or did you forget that I'm Or Shapira?"

"Damn you and Or Shapira. He's destroyed your common sense."

"Actually, Sheikh, he helped me get it back."

"Isn't that who you were impersonating at Sara'a? Do you want to ruin me?"

"I didn't use Or Shapira's identity there, no."

"Nur, do me a favor: don't lie to me. An inspector from the Ministry of Tourism came to Shakib with a complaint from some American tourist. They claimed you were shouting at them and cursing them and that you left them behind in the middle of nowhere. And that your name was Or Shapira . . . Shakib had no choice but to deny any prior knowledge of you. Did you really do that?"

"I don't know. Maybe . . . "

Now Sheikh Morsi pulled him back from his thoughts about the papers and the previous night, saying cautiously, "Tell me . . . are you sure about this plan of yours?"

Nur turned to him with a big smile and said, in Hebrew, "I am one hundred percent sure."

Sheikh Morsi stared at him, taken aback by Nur's self-confidence and his mastery of the Ashkenazi way of speaking, as well as his insistence on taking risks for the sake of telling Magdalene's story. Then he stood up to leave the room, wishing Nur luck and telling him, again, to eat.

But Nur had already gone back to scrutinizing his fabricated CV, which he felt, for a moment, lent legitimacy to his assumed persona, Or Shapira. Only a few hours separated him from putting on his mask to join the expedition at the Albright Institute. They were hours he would spend at the altar of his greatest love: Jerusalem. A Jerusalem in springtime filled with splendid rituals and wearing her Ramadan dress, embellished and illuminated with the most brilliant colours and lights.

* * *

Shortly before iftar, Sheikh Morsi invited him to join his family at the Ramadan table. Nur sat on the floor next to Sheikh Morsi and his wife, Zainab, who radiated generosity and motherliness, along with their seven children, ranging from the oldest, twenty-year-old Mohieddine, to the youngest, eleven-year-old Ezzedine. Nur had always wondered how Zainab, a slight forty-year-old, had been able to give birth to an entire Jerusalemite tribe. The table was groaning beneath the most delicious foods: a Ramadan spread par excellence. The star of the show was qudra, its rice, lamb, and locally made ghee fortified with chickpeas and garlic cloves. The series of plates was punctuated by carafes of juice—carob, licorice, and tamarind—bowls of salad and yogurt, and a delicious vegetable soup.

Agate prayer beads in hand, Sheikh Morsi was humbly praising God and seeking his forgiveness right up until the adhan sounded. As soon as he stood upright on the other side of the room to pray, his little tribe stood as one and lined up behind him in a scene overflowing with humility and faith. Nur listened in silent awe to Sheikh Morsi's voice as he recited the Holy Quran, that reassuring chant that made Nur feel at peace, a few moments of worship followed by licorice juice to slake their thirst, then food and more drink, as the table rang with the clattering of spoons and the joyful tumult of the children eating iftar. But Nur didn't apply himself to his meal with the same appetite; he was flustered and shy, even though he had slept, eaten, and drunk dozens of times at Sheikh Morsi's home. His mentor attempted to smooth out his embarrassment by ladling food onto his plate and encouraging him to eat, but only Nur really understood where his confused sense of discomfort stemmed from. He'd never known this kind of intimacy in his own home, in the folds of the camp. He'd never known this kind of family—children, siblings, father, mother, noise. A normal family. He'd never felt it. He wondered if this was what a family was supposed to look like. Was this how you were supposed to be as a father? As a mother? Was it supposed to have this touch of the divine?

After the mouth-watering iftar, Nur and Sheikh Morsi withdrew to the formal parlor next to the living room, praising Zainab's cooking as they went. She rewarded them moments later with delicious atayef stuffed with cream and nuts and accompanied by Sheikh Morsi's Ajamy tobacco argileh.

The sheikh wrested him away from this family atmosphere he'd never experienced at home. "If you're planning to go to the institute tomorrow, you should go early . . . 8 or 9 A.M., before the confrontations and the demonstrations start to heat up."

Nur responded quietly. "That's the plan."

"I told you, Nur, the situation's rough right now. Jerusalem hasn't witnessed an escalation like this in years. That's why I think you should stay in tonight . . . Don't go out walking around the Old City."

"Things are really that bad?"

"Worse than you can imagine, especially for a kid like you, wavering between Nur and Or." The comment stung, and Sheikh Morsi bandaged the wound he'd inflicted. "I mean, how could you go out tonight? If you go to Damascus Gate looking like that, people will think you're Jewish. And if a border guard asks for your ID, he'll want to know what a good Jewish boy is doing surrounded by Arabs. That's why I think you should stay home for now. But don't worry, when I'm back from Tarawih prayers at Al-Aqsa, we can chat till it's time for suhoor."

Nur retreated to his room sadly. "Okay, then . . . I'll work on my notes for the novel till you're back."

Sheikh Morsi's worry about him wandering through the Old City was enough to convince him to stay in, but it was a disappointing reminder that he still wasn't free. In the camp, his cell was built from the alleyways; here in Jerusalem, it was built from occupation, repression, and assault. But what could he do about it?

He stretched out on the bed, trying to shake off his disappointment by recording a new voice memo.

[APRIL 21 – JERUSALEM, EVENING:
TECHNICAL / ARTISTIC ASPECTS]

Along with fleshing out my knowledge of Magdalene's historical and religious context after the crucifixion, I need to establish the specifics of the Naseem Shakr timeline and learn about all the places he'll be moving through. On the to-do list:

1. Research the oldest church in Jerusalem.
2. Visit the Church of Mary Magdalene to see its treasures.
3. Visit the Rockefeller Museum to further examine its first-century Roman archaeological finds.

4. Ask Sheikh Morsi for stories about treasure and caves on the Mount of Olives.
5. Look into the possibility that there are secret Gnostic churches and monasteries in Jerusalem.

I've got to visit historical, religious, and archaeological sites, too, as much as possible, especially the ones linked to Jesus and Mary Magdalene . . . The most important of these are in Galilee, where the ruins of Capernaum, Nain, Magdala, and Nazareth are located. There wouldn't be any harm in another visit to Mount Carmel, either, just to fuel the imagination . . . Plus delving into Jerusalem's Biblical sites, like the Via Dolorosa and its stations, and imagining Magdalene there . . . Oh, and visiting the Church of the Holy Sepulchre and the Garden Tomb. But the most important historical site to visit is the ruins of the depopulated village of Al-Lajjun, southwest of Tel Megiddo.

PS: Murad . . . I forgot to tell you: I don't know if I'll make it back to the camp before your mother's next visit. If I don't manage to get her the two books you asked for, please forgive me . . . I'll buy them tomorrow, here in Jerusalem, and I'll leave them with Sheikh Morsi until I get back, after the dig season.

He turned off his phone before Sheikh Morsi got back from Tarawih. He couldn't stomach the idea of a pleasant chat on this night Jerusalem had expelled him from, confining him instead to a room filled with the toxic smoke of gas bombs and the noise of stun grenades heralding the nightly clashes between Jerusalem's youth and the border police. Then, suddenly, he leapt back out of bed and turned the light on. He stood in front of the mirror and looked himself in the eye before saying, with every ounce of determination and steadiness he possessed: "Good morning. I'm Or . . . Or Shapira."

* * *

He got up at 8 A.M. and took an energizing shower, then stole quietly back to his room, careful not to disturb the sleeping house.

He dressed in his favorite pair of light-wash jeans and a white linen shirt, then stepped into his gray shoes, styling his hair in the mirror before pulling it back with a white hair tie. He spritzed his Cacharel cologne into the air in front of him and stepped into the fragrant mist, feeling it disperse across his body and add to his appeal. He contemplated his features in the mirror for a few moments, then grabbed his phone off the table to change the language from Arabic to Hebrew; every little detail would matter now. He sat down on the edge of the bed to quickly catch up on the latest news, starting with an Arabic news agency:

DOZENS OF PROTESTERS INJURED IN JERUSALEM AFTER RIGHT-WING SETTLERS RAID THE BLESSED AL-AQSA MOSQUE

Then he clicked over to a Zionist news site to continue his rounds:

DOZENS OF RIOTERS ESCALATE VIOLENCE AND DISTURBANCE OF THE PEACE IN JERUSALEM

ATTORNEY GENERAL REFUSES TO ISSUE LEGAL OPINION ON EVICTION NOTICES IN SHIMON HATZEDIK

He withdrew from his electronic news roundup, making do with these two items that agreed on the escalating tensions in Jerusalem but differed on the motives, names, and categories. The Jerusalemite protesting the desecration of his city's holy place became a rioter and a provocateur, the Sheikh Jarrah neighborhood became Shimon HaTzedik, and on this cautiously peaceful morning, Nur al-Shahdi became Or Shapira.

He checked for his fake ID, then took the gold Star of David necklace from a small pocket in his bag, put it on, and tucked it under the collar of his shirt, where it would stay while he was in the Old City; later, he would display it on his chest, flaunting his Zionist Jewish features.

He looked at himself in the mirror for the last time as he put on a pair of sunglasses rimmed in thin gold wire. He sighed deeply, grabbed his file folder stuffed with the details of his new identity, and left.

He walked out of the courtyard gate and descended the stone steps leading to Silsila; a trickle of passersby gave him confidence, reassuring him. Then he turned left. Up to this point, Nur was still Nur, no more, no less.

He glanced around as he walked; some shops in the souq were still closed, and other shopkeepers yawned lazily on their way to open their doors in pursuit of a livelihood. He reached the turn leading north to Al-Wad Street and strolled along it. He felt that Jerusalem in all her splendor was accompanying him, arm in arm, as if he were wandering through poems about her and to her; this was his covenant with her, that he would imagine her in order to embrace and love her. He savored the morning calm that had settled after the turmoil of the previous night's bullets, gas, and stun grenades.

He took another turn, a right this time, heading east along the Via Dolorosa, that road that Jesus walked, collapsing several times from the effects of torture and the heavy burden of his cross. Nur had always walked this path as a tour guide for groups of pilgrims and foreign tourists; now he walked it carrying his mask rather than his cross, wondering whether all the roads and paths of Jerusalem weren't just as crowded with pain.

He crossed the halfway point of his walk, then turned left, heading north. The road leading to Herod's Gate was usually quiet and empty of pedestrians at this time of day, unlike Damascus Gate, which tended to be heavily guarded by police and border guards.

He ended his morning ramble through the Old City there, at Herod's Gate . . . He didn't go out the way he came in, as Nur al-Shahdi, but rather as Or Shapira, who put on his sunglasses and looked around without arousing any suspicion, then uncovered the gold Star of David on his chest and crossed to the opposite side of the street, heading toward the broad expanse of Salah ed-Din Street, which was lined with shops, residential buildings, and various institutions, prominent among them the W.F. Albright Institute of Archaeological Research.

"Or . . . Or Shapira" walked confidently along the sidewalk. He would've liked to leave the Old City through Damascus Gate and take Sultan Sulayman Street, using its southern sidewalk as a platform from which to contemplate Jerusalem's towering wall on this dazzling April morning, glancing over at the entrance to the cave famously known as King Solomon's Quarries, which he'd entered more than once with his tourists, dreaming of diving into its secret corridors and legendary tales. But this morning, and with his new identity, he preferred to avoid arousing suspicion or attracting attention, so he continued along Salah ed-Din until he reached his destination. On his right, the huge stone building was covered with a tiled roof that confirmed its age—more than a hundred years old—and was complemented by a lush garden adorned with pine, cypress, and eucalyptus trees. Next to it was a large open square, part of it in use as a parking lot for the institute's employees and visitors.

He stopped in front of the gate for a few moments, not because he was hesitant but just to confirm he wasn't dreaming. Then he crossed the threshold, entering a foyer that led to a big room lined with wooden benches and multiple doors. He noticed a small, glassed-in office to his right at the end of the room. Or made his way toward the woman sitting there, thinking she might be the institute's secretary. He greeted her in English with a "Good morning!" and punctuated his greeting with the name he'd been practicing since the night before, a Thursday. Then he asked her about the announcement regarding the archaeological expedition and its supervisor and was met with an automatic, American-style smile. She invited him to sit down and wait for Professor Brian Moore, the former curator of the Harvard Museum of the Ancient Near East and the general supervisor of the second dig season for the Roman Sixth Legion camp.

He waited with a composure borrowed from the splendid Or Shapira, quietly absorbed in all these first-time rituals, his manners of speech, and how he would open the conversation with the American professor. Nur expected the latter to be old, so he was surprised when the man who emerged from one of the hallway doors looked more like the legendary archaeologist himself, Indiana Jones, as played by Harrison Ford. Or Shapira stood up confidently and wished him a good morning in fluent English. The professor couldn't help but catch sight of the Star of David shining on Or's chest and greeted him cheerfully: "Come on, man . . . You waited till the very last day to sign up. We've been waiting for you!"

Nur was surprised by this cheery turn of events, but Or responded in turn: "My apologies, Professor, I was deep in the depths of Solomon's Mines, searching for his throne."

The professor had a booming laugh. "Please, Or, no titles . . . Call me Brian; I'm only a few years older than you."

Or was relieved by the joking tone Brian had adopted as a bridge for getting to know each other, removing the awkwardness and the burden of pleasantries. Brian invited him into his office to give him the details of the expedition and its dates. The questions in Nur's mind seemed to flow through Or on their way to him. *Is it my Hebrew name and the Star of David that prompted such a hearty welcome? What if I told you my name was Nur al-Shahdi—would you treat me the same?*

Then he passed Brian his resume, redolent with his perfect English and sweet little lies about his work as a tour guide all across the country over the past five years, in addition to his participation in many expeditions and excavation seasons in such spots as Jerusalem, Jericho, and Caesarea. He told Brian he was interested in this particular expedition because his thesis had been about the Bar Kokhba Revolt. The only lie involved in this aspect of his resume was the name of the university and the program, changing a degree in Islamic antiquities at Al-Quds University's Higher Institute of Archaeology to a degree from Tel Aviv University, which was built on the destroyed coastal village of Al-Shaykh Muwannis, depopulated during the Nakba. Brian seemed pleased: with him, with his career, maybe with his Zionist origins. He verified that Or had received the coronavirus vaccine and then briefed him on the details of the expedition, informing him that it would begin the following Monday, April 26, when several groups from prestigious European and American universities and institutes would meet at the Kibbutz Mishmar HaEmek, in addition to some graduates and researchers from Israeli archaeology departments. He added that room and board would be covered by the institute, the Israel Antiquities Authority, and the kibbutz, and emphasized that while several lectures on the Roman Sixth Legion and the history of the Tel Megiddo site had been scheduled at the institute, he'd decided to postpone them until all the members of the expedition were together at the kibbutz.

Or listened intently to Brian's briefing, which didn't seem to portend any challenges or obstacles, and finally Brian asked, in conclusion, "Are you free at the moment, or are you working?"

"I'm totally free!"

"Great! What would you think about joining us here at the institute for the next few days, till the expedition?"

"What would I be doing?"

"We have tasks for recent graduates and other volunteers, helping with stuff like cleaning potsherds and putting them back together. That sort of thing. Would you like to volunteer?"

Nur whispered in Or's ear, "Say no, say no; they'll figure it out."

Or responded, still brimming with confidence, "I would love to."

"Great! You can come tomorrow at 9 A.M. and work till 4 . . . Let me add you to the expedition's WhatsApp group now, and then I'll take you on a tour of the institute."

Nur muttered to Or, "Shit . . . Hold on tight, this is the first test . . . "

He entered the large laboratory filled with fragments of pottery and archaeological finds such as oil lamps, statuettes, and weapons from different historical periods. Brian led him toward a group of volunteers gathered around a long wooden table, busily gathering and numbering shards of earthenware jars. Brian greeted them encouragingly and then introduced Or, and they exchanged greetings with him—all in English except for one hello that pierced the air in Hebrew, falling from the mouth of a young woman standing next to them: "Hello . . . I'm Ayala Sharabi; I graduated recently from the Faculty of Archaeology at the Hebrew University."

Nur whispered into Or's ear, "Shit! Back away, back away from her. Don't speak Hebrew. One word pronounced with an Arabic accent might give you away . . . speak English!"

Or spoke up confidently, in his Ashkenazi Hebrew: "Nice to meet you, miss."

Ayala was of medium height, with short black hair and a few blonde highlights framing her pale, full-cheeked face, wide black eyes, and a nose that complemented her plump lips, which were in harmony with a healthy, attractive body. She'd covered the latter with tight gray trousers, their seductive nature softened by the loose blue shirt protecting her chest and the charms of her twenty-three years.

A long stare from Or was followed by a whispered curse from Nur, who demanded that Or follow Brian to another, smaller table that had two young men and two young women crowded around it, busy reassembling the bones of a skeleton found at one of the dig sites. With continued enthusiasm, Brian pointed out the two young men. "That's Tony and John; they're specialists from George Washington University's Capitol Archaeological Institute." He gestured at the women. "And these two lovelies, Emily and Nicole, are experts in archaeological restoration. They've come from Brussels to figure out where this mysterious skeleton came from. You can join them tomorrow, if you like."

"Of course, of course."

He shook their hands warmly as he spoke, and introduced himself, relieved not to have been caught off guard by another Hebrew greeting like the one Ayala had sprung on him.

They left the lab, and Brian led him toward the institute's library, which Nur had always heard about and whose abundance he'd dreamed of examining. The library was estimated to hold more than thirty-five thousand of the most important texts in history and archaeology.

Brian interrupted Nur's astonishment at the library's scope and stateliness. "Please excuse me, Or; I have an online meeting with two colleagues from Harvard . . . But feel free to wander around and browse the library to your heart's content. I'll see you tomorrow!"

If I were Nur, would he have left me alone here, with no supervision, no guards . . .?

The library enticed him with its stillness and emptiness, and with the smell of old paper and leather. He didn't know where to start exploring, or which books would add new richness to his novel. Which details would dazzle him? He pulled himself together and controlled his excitement over disappearing into the stacks for two hours, the minutes and seconds hurrying past as he flipped through a book here and a volume there, not daring to record a single voice memo, despite Nur's insistence.

* * *

He left the institute in mid-afternoon like someone waking up from a deep dream. He gasped for air, catching the breath that had been stolen from him in the corridors of the institute. This was the first time he'd fully assumed his new identity, a face in an Ashkenazi mask with a purely Hebrew name, since he'd first found the ID three years before. He'd never worn it, uttered it, revealed it, as he had a short while earlier. And now here he was on Salah ed-Din Street in the middle of the day, with the traffic of pedestrians and cars swarming around him, searching for his next step. This was where his path led now: forward.

In Jerusalem, he wouldn't go back to being Nur al-Shahdi, though he reinstated him now, hiding the Star of David inside his shirt.

He was about to return to the Old City but suddenly stopped and turned back when he remembered Murad's last request for books. He went to a bookstore that was just a few steps away on the same street. He had visited it often to obtain books and journals specializing in his dual fields.

He entered the bookstore. It was empty aside from its owner, Abu Ibrahim, who was combating the boredom of his day by rearranging books, lining them up on the shelves to dispel his afternoon drowsiness and the thirst caused by fasting. When he saw Nur, he greeted him warmly: "Nur! Well, hello! Where have you been? I haven't seen you for ages."

He tossed out his name so suddenly, when Nur had just been immersed in his identity as Or Shapira, that he looked around cautiously, as though the man's greeting might have somehow reached the ears of the institute residents. Then, calm again, he responded, "Ramadan Kareem, 'Aami . . . As you know, it's gotten harder to move around lately. Things are so tense."

He then hurried to ask Abu Ibrahim for the two books Murad wanted, and the bookseller thought for a moment and scanned his shelves before replying: "*Culture and Imperialism* by Edward Said is available, but *Postcolonial Studies*, well . . . I can order it for you, but it'll take some time."

"That's okay."

He thanked Abu Ibrahim and then, as usual, headed toward the section with the historical books and those specializing in archaeological research and adventure tales, immersing himself in the titles and flipping through a few texts as Abu Ibrahim went back to his shop.

"You'll put me back on soon . . . don't enjoy this return to your roots too much," Or whispered in Nur's ear, and the latter responded in his own whisper: "I'll put you on whenever and however I like; *you* don't make the rules."

"I'll expose you . . . I'll tell the bookstore owner you're a fraud, that you're impersonating someone you're not . . . someone Jewish."

"Are you an actual Zionist or just Jewish?"

"What's the difference?"

"There's a huge difference . . . I don't think Abu Ibrahim and I would have an issue with you being Jewish, but a Zionist . . . "

"Really, Mr. Philosopher? You wanna go straight to the nit-picky terminology?"

"That's where the problem is: in the terminology and the details . . . Now hush and let me focus."

What was wrong with him? Why was he wavering between Nur and Or? He'd been in this uncertain state since morning. A possessed, mad exchange of whispers between them. Nur and Or, Or and Nur. He was alarmed by what was happening to him. He left the shelves of the bookstore and Abu Ibrahim behind after agreeing to return soon to purchase both books together.

Where to now?

Soon, Jerusalem would erupt in clashes and escalations between her people and the Zionist border guards.

He decided to return to Silsila. Leaving Salah ed-Din Street, he turned right, preferring to return via Sultan Sulayman Street, taking the southern sidewalk opposite the Jerusalem city wall, a quiet, sparsely populated walk.

Silence, accompanied by the smooth flow of cars and other vehicles in both directions, granted the sidewalk a certain intimacy and prompted Nur to sit down on one of its metal benches, where he could slow his breathing and rest a little from the adrenaline produced by his adventure. He pulled out his phone, preparing to record some new information Or had obtained from the institute's library.

[THURSDAY, APRIL 22 – JERUSALEM, AFTERNOON –
MARY MAGDALENE'S GNOSTICISM]

In Elaine Pagels's study, *The Gnostic Gospels*, she reviews excerpts from some Gnostic texts. The Gospel of Philip, which was banned by the Church, provides a focal point we can use to examine Magdalene in all her dimensions: mystical, Gnostic, and spiritual.

. . . the companion of the [Savior is] Mary Magdalene. [But Christ loved] her more than [all] the disciples, and used to kiss her [often] on her [mouth]. The rest of [the disciples were offended] . . . They said to him, "Why do you love her more than all of us?" The Savior answered and said to them, "Why do I not love you as [I love] her?"

This paragraph sheds light on the relationship between Magdalene and Jesus, keeping in mind that, generally speaking, the Gnostic gospels don't document Jesus's mission chronologically but, instead, record spiritual teachings that emphasize Jesus's relationship with his disciples and the effect it had on them—especially on Peter.

Unlike Dan Brown, though, I'm not saying Jesus was married

to Magdalene. What I'm saying is that they were brought together by a Gnostic, spiritual relationship. They're a single reality with two dimensions, one male and one female, and the kiss, or the ritual of kissing they practiced, as mentioned in the Gospel of Philip, isn't sexual; it's spiritual. If Jesus wanted to kiss Magdalene with an intimate, sexual kiss, would he have done it in plain view and within earshot of his twelve disciples and other followers and believers?

I believe that in Gnostic rituals, kisses signify secret knowledge, imparted in whispers. Kisses are doctrine . . . the kiss is the commandment.

PS: Dear Murad,

Here I am, sitting in front of the walls of Jerusalem on an April afternoon in Ramadan . . . I don't know if Jerusalem will reflect back my shadow or Or's . . . Or, who, as soon as I assumed his character and put on his mask, burst from within me and began walking by my side . . . He, like me, has no shadow—at least not yet.

Murad, I don't know what's happening to me. Today I discovered my acting potential . . . I feel like I deserve the Oscar for best actor. And Or deserves one for best supporting actor. Or maybe vice-versa . . .

Today I was fearless, experienced and capable, and totally at ease. But who is it that's fearless, really—me or Or?

* * *

"Shakib was in a good mood today, so I took advantage of it and talked to him about you. I didn't tell him you were staying at my house, obviously . . . But I'm happy to announce that he's agreed for you to come back to work—just in Bethlehem this time. What do you think?"

Nur shrugged, resigned. "Thanks for trying to help . . . but I'm not going back to work for the agency, not here or at any other branch."

Sheikh Morsi looked taken aback. Somewhat sharply, he asked, "So what *will* you do? Are you going to keep acting like a madman forever? Even if things went well for you at the institute today, they might go badly at Mishmar HaEmek."

"Just be patient with this madman for a bit, Sheikh; don't worry too much about him." Nur sounded hurt.

"I'm nervous for you . . . A young man of your age and talents shouldn't be fumbling about like this in the dark."

Sheikh Morsi stood up, on his way out for Tarawih prayers at Al-Aqsa, as usual. Nur stopped him, his voice rasping painfully. "Won't you take me with you to pray at Al-Aqsa? I miss visiting the Haram al-Sharif."

The sheikh turned toward him, sighing heavily. "And how will you get in? With which look, which ID? As Nur or Or?" He closed the door behind him, leaving in his wake two figures and a single trembling shadow in an ancient Jerusalem room. Whose shadow was trembling now—Nur's or Or's?

Nur threw himself onto the bed, his mind wandering, contemplating what had happened to him that day at the institute, where he had laid the foundation for his breakthrough and where all signs currently pointed to success. Then, suddenly, Or attacked, his whisper frightening: "You're not the one who convinced Brian to accept you on the dig. It was me . . . After all, I'm Or Shapira, not you, right? Tell me, what's your name? Who are you?"

"Does someone like you even care what someone like me is called? You guys decided what my name would be a long time ago . . . That's what my friend says—my friend whose name you also picked out: terrorist and provocateur . . . Intruder illegally present in Israel."

"Why are you overcomplicating things? I just asked what your name was."

"Or Shapira."

"Son of a bitch, now you're a wise guy? Are you forgetting that you assaulted my identity? *You* impersonated *me*!"

"Yeah, you were suffering *so* much from the luxury of your ID that you somehow left it in the pocket of your leather jacket."

"You're wearing my leather jacket, too?"

"I got it at the flea market."

"Um, okay. Now what?"

"Now what?"

"I'm asking what you want from me. When do I get a break from your insanity?"

"When you give me a break from yours!"

Nur jumped out of bed as though he'd been stung—what had just happened? What was wrong?

He headed to the window, opening it and inhaling the mild Jerusalem air, thinking it might bring him back to himself. He contemplated the scene before him, the city at night. He looked lovingly at the golden dome that crowned the rock, recalling a hadith Sheikh Morsi had once quoted for him during a tour on the Haram al-Sharif: "God Almighty said to the rock of Jerusalem: 'In you is my heaven and my hell; in you is my reward and my punishment. So blessed is he who looks upon you; blessed is he who looks upon you; blessed is he who looks upon you.'"

Chapter 4

It's absurd to want to prove the historicity of Mary Magdalene . . . But that doesn't mean we shouldn't believe that she was there beside Jesus in the Gospels. As St. Augustine says, "I believe because it is absurd."

So my text won't try to prove that Magdalene was real. Instead, it will engage with the historical and religious information we have about her, which should make for an interesting, exciting novel. The deeper I delve into the details of the era, the more I get lost, and the more I find myself entering frightening worlds and going down hidden corridors, ultimately—hopefully—to emerge with a good awareness of that time. Because I can't write without a thorough understanding of the first century AD . . .

As for the historical existence of Magdalene, there's a story referenced in the book *The Golden Legend* that confirms that Mary Magdalene was from the castle of Magdalo, which is the village of Magdala or Al-Majdal. Both parents came from a noble lineage, her father Cyrus and her mother Eucharis; hers was a wealthy family. As for how Magdalene became linked to the vial of perfume she anointed Jesus's feet with, there's a strange incident mentioned in "The Arabic Infancy Gospel of the Savior" under the title "Story of the Blessed Virgin Mary": And the time of circumcision, that is, the eighth day, being at hand, the child was to be circumcised according to the law.

Wherefore they circumcised Him in the cave. And the old Hebrew woman took the piece of skin; but some say that she took the navel-string, and laid it past in a jar of old oil of nard. And she had a son, a dealer in unguents, and she gave it to him, saying: See that thou do not sell this jar of unguent of nard, even although three hundred denarii should be offered thee for it.[3]

This is the jar that Mary, the sinful woman, purchased, as per Luke 8:37-38, and poured over Jesus. And this brings me back to the need to deconstruct the idea of a "sinful woman" based on the popular civic vision of the period, emphasizing that Magdalene appears in the Gospel of Luke *after* the story of the sinful woman from Nain . . . If the concept of a "sinful woman," in the popular expression of the time, meant a prostitute or adulteress, what could motivate a woman to engage in prostitution other than poverty? And Magdalene was from a wealthy family . . .

What I'm assuming here is that Magdalene violated the norms of the world she lived in by disobeying Jewish laws that weren't part of the fabric of Galilee the way they were of the Jerusalem area. As far as the Jewish legal system was concerned, Galilee was, after all, the "Galilee of the Gentiles."

Magdalene went against the grain by joining a secret society or brotherhood that used caves on Mount Carmel as a refuge for secret Gnostic worship . . . There, Mary Magdalene received the commandments and illumination. Maybe she was practicing some sacred sexual ritual in which knowledge and insight united to form the true, illuminated Word, and after gaining that knowledge, Magdalene joined Jesus though the ritual of pouring perfume on his feet and body in Nain or Bethany.

[3] "The Arabic Infancy Gospel of the Savior," as cited in Alexander Roberts, Sir James Donaldson, Arthur Cleveland Coxe, *Ante-Nicene Fathers*, vol. 8 (1886), http://www.gnosis.org/library/infarab.htm.

It's worth pointing out that mountains have symbolic meanings and are mentioned in the four gospels as places of worship, meeting, and transfiguration—especially the mountains of Galilee. There's more than one mountain where Jesus is supposed to have met with his disciples; among them was Mount Tabor near Nazareth, and maybe also Mount Megiddo, or Harmageddon. Mount Carmel, as a secret temple, might have been the meeting place referred to in the Gospel of Matthew: "Now the eleven disciples went to Galilee, to the mountain to which Jesus had directed them. And when they saw him they worshiped him [. . .]" (Matthew 28:16-17).

I don't know . . . It feels like I'm drowning in the details . . . Weighing the texts down with an interpretation too heavy for them to bear.

PS: My friend . . . Do you miss my voice? I miss hearing it through your ears. I haven't poured my heart out to you for three days. And no, please don't tell me I've been too distracted volunteering at the institute. It's more complicated than that. I already told you, this is the first time I've breathed to the rhythm of Or Shapira's long, rapid breaths, and it's been exhausting. I've been so anxious, like I might accidentally reveal my identity before even really getting started. At any rate, tomorrow, my friend, is the day I head off to the expedition headquarters in Mishmar HaEmek. I'll be taking the bus, alone; Ayala begged me to ride with her in her car, but I got out of it.

Oh, Murad . . . I can just see you griping now, complaining about me dropping her name so casually without any reservations or social niceties. Ayala . . . you know how her name translates to Arabic, don't you?

She really is a gazelle, my friend . . . Please don't misunderstand; you know me, I'm the same as I've always been, anointed with the same insurmountable purity as always. It was and still is a faithful guardian . . . But I've gotta admit that she's rich material for masturbation . . . I mean, why not—why not think of her as I practice my secret habit? Why not? As a people, we're better at masturbating than practically anyone else, anywhere. The entire nation spills its energies down the drains . . . It's the only time we use our imaginations properly.

And don't even think about accusing me of normalization now! What normalization? Have you forgotten that I'm Or Shapira? If I hadn't been wearing my mask, sure, *then* it would have been normalization.

She stood next to me at the wooden table today as I helped the two Belgian specialists, Emily and Nicole, reassemble the skeleton . . . She stood there, straight as an arrow, and seared Or (not me) with the nearness of her breath. I was absorbed in the necklace dangling over the junction of her breasts, which seemed to stare back at me seductively. A silver necklace in the shape of Palestine. Imagine, Murad, it's the same map, the same shape, that you sent me from prison, carved from a domino tile. I almost ripped it off her neck and shouted, "This is mine! This country is mine! How can you wear something that isn't yours?"

Then I started comparing the value she gave the necklace with my own map . . . The national and patriotic, historical, cultural, geographical, and religious value of it . . . Is there a difference between the two other than that this map is made of silver and the other one's a domino? Please don't get angry . . . Don't tell me I got pushed toward sexual normalization the second some glistening cleavage pressed itself against me in front of a skeleton. No, Murad . . . It's all in the details—remember?

And before I forget, I should tell you that Ayala's a Sephardic Jew . . . Her features were a clue, and she confirmed as much during the break when she told me her family was of Syrian origin, from Aleppo, and that she lived in Ramat Gan, which isn't far from Tel Aviv.

On my first day volunteering, my Ashkenazi Hebrew, with all its *kha* sounds, was at the ready, fully mobilized for my first victory over Ayala, who, noticing my friendliness and compatibility with Nicole and Emily, later whispered to me that they were lesbians . . . She threw it out there in a sexy Hebrew to save me the trouble of trying to seduce them—even though the thought hadn't crossed my mind. I wasn't there to make some puffed up, macho gesture to try and finagle them both into one of the institute's beds. She said, "They're both lesbians, but please don't think I'm against gay rights . . . Of course not; I think they should have full rights." And I thought, as Nur al-Shahdi, *So you support gay rights . . . but the rights of an entire people to life and freedom—not so much?*

Deep down, I was condemning her liberal notions even though, in reality, I didn't know anything about her attitude toward me—me the Palestinian, son of a tormented refugee people.

The girl got up in my face, Murad. I wasn't ready for it when she started peppering me with all the usual Hebrew questions. Where do you live? What do you do? Where did you serve in the army? Where's your family from originally? Who do you vote for in the Knesset?

I responded with all the high-handed Ashkenazi reserve and displeasure I could muster, and she backed off some, grumbling a little flirtatiously, "You Ashkenazim have always treated us Sephardim like we're less than you . . . *You're* the masters of Israel; *you* liberated it from the Arabs and built it up. You serve in the most elite combat units. And *we*'re just a bunch of animals, at least according to one of your artist types . . . "

She looked me in my Ashkenazi face, practically quivering, and told me, half-kidding, somewhere between cordiality and hatred, that leftists like me were the ones voting for Meretz or the Labor Party. People like *me* were the ones who persecuted Arab Jews by sticking them in transit camps when the state was first established and then, after Zionist reeducation, pushing them into developing towns and cities on the margins. Making Tel Aviv the center of Ashkenazi dominance.

"For God's sake, Ayala. Give it a rest with the Sephardic outrage."

"I'm just teasing you, Or . . .! I know you're not an Ashkenazi bigot."

Then I drew her into a conversation about our expedition, history, and archaeology . . . distancing myself from the predicament she'd put me in with her ample chest.

We were chatting, the two of us, Nicole, Emily, and a few other students, as we devoured the pizza Brian had brought us, the edges of our conversation overlapping with the sounds of the clashes raging in the square beside Damascus Gate and spilling out onto Sultan Sulayman and Salah ed-Din Streets as Friday prayers ended. As the people of Jerusalem demonstrated to defend the sanctity of their holy sites, homes, and public spaces against the demolitions and settlements that sought to gradually erase them, we chatterboxes ignored the echoing chants, whistles, stun grenades, and bullets around us. It didn't concern Ayala, so why should it concern me; I'd already begun to conform, albeit unwillingly, to Or Shapira's Zionist safety measures.

The institute was an island isolated from its turbulent surroundings . . . No one in it cared about what was happening outside. Or so most of us pretended . . . Ladies and gentlemen, quiet, please, we're working with the bowels of the earth; we have nothing to do with what happens up above. We'll intervene once you're buried in its womb, you and all your belongings, your memories and treasures; we'll excavate the earth for your traces hundreds of years from now . . . But me, Nur al-Shahdi, I haven't died yet, Murad. Please don't say I have . . . Don't announce my death now and rush me off to the abode of madness and absence. I'm a living monument, aren't I? One more than seventy years old.

Isn't that what you told me in one of your smuggled letters? Hang on a second, let me remember exactly what it was you wrote . . . You said, "It's a shame we commemorate the Nakba every year like it's just some historical event. The Nakba's not over yet . . . It's still fertile, capable of giving birth any second. And what it gives birth to is murder, displacement, ethnic cleansing, dispossession, destruction, marginalization, discrimination, obfuscation, and false peace." That's what you said.

By the way . . . I'm guessing you've heard that the Palestinian Authority's different factions are planning to hold legislative elections now, after fourteen-plus years of bitter internal strife . . . You might've also heard that the number of independents participating in those elections is higher than the number of people affiliated with the parties. What kind of nonsense is that? Isn't *that* normalization, Mr. Colonialism-Is-in-the-Details?

He rubbed his face with his palms and turned over on the bed. He would be there soon . . . deep in the Zionist heartland: Kibbutz Mishmar HaEmek. Every last thing was ready: the language, his features, the ID, his clothes for the dig.

This was his last night in Jerusalem, and he couldn't close his eyes, not even for a short nap to escape the turmoil of anticipation. This was a kibbutz. Not just any kibbutz, but one of the oldest socialist Zionist ones, and it was waiting for him. Waiting for a young Palestinian refugee in his finest Ashkenazi attire to chase after a bygone history in Tel Megiddo and Al-Lajjun and perhaps reveal something about Mary Magdalene. He wouldn't get a chance to sleep later: Sheikh Morsi had promised to stop by his room to say goodbye, as befits close friends, before he left the following afternoon.

He tossed and turned, finally settling on his left side, facing the mirror. He stared at his reflection for a few moments before Or emerged from the mirror, snickering, and whispered, "Scared?"

"I mean . . . yeah. Aren't you?"

"I'm not scared . . . I'm pissed."

"Why?"

"Because you're talking about Ayala like she's about to strip naked in front of you and let you take her. Is it because she's Jewish that you think she's some horny prostitute in need of a hard Arab dick?"

"No . . . It's not like that."

"It *is* like that, and more. Yeah, Ayala's hot; she's got that Eastern beauty men can't get enough of—all men, not just Arabs or Ashkenazim—but that doesn't give you the right to talk about her like she and her big juicy titties are all over you."

"Don't you want her?"

"What?"

"When she's close to you at the institute, doesn't her breath on your neck feel like fire?"

"So now you wanna give me a lesson in seducing women? You, the naïve idiot who's never touched a woman in his life. Yes, you could've had her at the institute, but not because she's Jewish and you're a Palestinian refugee. Because she's a hottie who would be a good match for a handsome guy like you—I mean, me."

"What would you do if you were me?"

"I would make it a point to prove juuuust how important the Zionist melting pot is for the Sephardi-Ashkenazi union . . . I'd get her under me and make her forget she ever thought we Ashkenazim viewed Sephardic Jews as inferior."

"Okay. So how would you fuck her?"

"Trying to steal my imagination now, asshole? Aren't you sick of your own hand yet? Now you want the spank bank of an Ashkenazi. You want to know how Or Shapira would fuck Ayala Sharabi!"

"No—I don't need that. It's enough to know I'll be fucking your mask in a little while."

"Fuck you."

"No, fuck you."

* * *

[SUNDAY, APRIL 25: JERUSALEM, BEFORE MIDNIGHT]

Was Magdalene the disciple Jesus loved?

There's some haziness surrounding the identity of the "disciple Jesus loved," who's mentioned multiple times in the four gospels. Some say it was John the son of Zebedee, the fisherman, and others say it was Lazarus, whom Jesus raised from the dead. There's also a reference to the disciple Jesus loved reclining against his chest during the Last Supper. They said that this disciple would never die but would stay alive until Jesus returned to save humanity.

I disagree with Dan Brown's distorted view in *The Da Vinci Code*, that Leonardo Da Vinci's *Last Supper* is a reference to Magdalene as the Holy Grail holding the sacred royal blood of Jesus. But I do think that the disciple Jesus loved, across all the gospels and Gnostic gospels, is none other than Mary Magdalene. And I can prove it, using an analysis of one of the Gnostic texts, the Secret Gospel of Mark.

In *The Gospel's Riddles*, Firas al-Sawwah talks about researcher Morton Smith's 1957 discovery of a paper glued to the cover of a seventeenth-century theological book at the Monastery of Mar Saba, southeast of Jerusalem, where the monks regularly made covers for new books from old papers and scrolls. This particular paper was a letter in Greek from the theologian Clement of Alexandria in the mid-second century AD to a Palestinian clergyman named Theodore. In a previous letter, he'd asked him about the existence of a Secret Gospel of Mark that differed from the official one in circulation. This secret gospel was used by a Gnostic sect known as the Carpocratians (after their teacher Carpocrates, who lived in Alexandria in the first century AD). They believed that the soul would stay trapped in the cycle of reincarnation if it didn't repay its debt to the world by enjoying all life's pleasures, especially the sexual ones.

This secret gospel also told a story about Jesus resurrecting a young man from Bethany; the resurrection ended with a ritual retreat in which Jesus granted the youth, who came to him alone and wearing only a light cloth over his naked body, the secrets of the divine light. Theodore pointed out that this story wasn't in the other gospels, and Clement replied that Mark had written two gospels: the first, exoteric one was the older of the two, recorded in approximately 70 AD. The other one was a secret, spiritual, esoteric text directed at those who were fully immersed in the mysteries of religion. In addition, Mark had received secret teachings from Jesus, a goal of which was to guide followers to the Holy of Holies of truth. Clement told Theodore that they couldn't tell people every truth and that they had to refute the Carpocratians under oath, denying that Mark was the author of this gospel.

If I compare this gospel with the text about Jesus kissing Mary Magdalene and the disciples' complaints about him favoring her, it seems to me that the intimacy of this ritual union was not between two men but between a man as insight and a woman as knowledge—as Sophia, or wisdom—so that they might appear together, united in the word of the illuminated gnosis . . . That's why I assume Magdalene was the disciple Jesus loved and that after Jesus filled her heart with light and knowledge, she transformed into Sophia, who is neither woman nor man . . .

I don't know. Maybe!

PS: Murad, I'm still here in Jerusalem, inside an ancient room that, a little while ago, was bubbling over with Sheikh Morsi's generosity and friendship: one last chat before Mishmar HaEmek.

On which note, let me tell you what he did for me yesterday

. . . When he got back from Tarawih prayers, he decided to take me to one of the Sufi zawiyas the Old City is teeming with, and we took streets and alleys I'd never set foot on during my tours in Jerusalem. We walked deeper, surrounded by stone arches on all sides, and I realized that Jerusalem is his, his alone; he's the bridegroom, not me, and the city's the bride who reveals her secrets to those who hold her, adore her, and praise her names with humility and supplication. I thought I loved her as much as he did, only to realize when she enfolded us in her luminous embrace that no, he loves her more.

Before we turned into the last alleyway leading to a two-story stone house with a low, narrow entrance, he said, "Think of this as compensation since you can't visit Al-Aqsa now, while the Occupation's making so much trouble. Just be sincere in your intentions. Enter the zawiya as Nur, lover of light, no more or less."

The zawiya's Sufi warmth, blended with its dignity and nobility, touched me. As soon as we passed through the narrow door, a vast courtyard opened out from the low entryway. Drawing me into the depths of the zawiya was the keening of a cane flute played with heart by a man draped in a turquoise-green mantle, standing erect but humble in the center of a large dhikr circle, dozens of worshippers sitting around him, attuned to the sweet melody he played.

We joined the circle as the worshippers moved to make space for us, their voices combined into a single whisper, repeating supplications and prayers.

"O Compassionate, O Benevolent . . . O Possessor of Light and Honor . . ."

The whispering harmonized with the flute, and the flautist began to turn around himself slowly in a dance that kept rhythm with his melodies. Then his dancing and playing quickened as the whisper became a chant sung out by a single loud, unified voice. The worshippers stood, including Sheikh Morsi and me, and we clasped hands and began to circle the flautist. The chanting intensified, and to be honest, Murad, I didn't feel the same strange sense of union they evidently did in the merging of the whisper and clamor, the wailing of the flute, the dance, the panting, and the lean, trembling bodies. I was only copying them, seeking humility and union like they were, but I failed. Maybe my heart wasn't distilling the spirit of Sufism; maybe I had traces of Or inside me. I don't know . . .

The dancing and chanting lasted for more than an hour, during which time those who were tired would occasionally withdraw to get some rest, spreading out on the ground along the walls, and I seized the opportunity to escape from the grip of Sheikh Morsi and another worshipper, contemplating from afar this Sufi circle eager for devotion and luminous unity, until the playing, dancing, and chanting stopped with a cry from an old sheikh who seemed to be the axis of the circle: "O Living One, O Manifest One, we wonder, and we wander."

Then he ordered the worshippers, who were splayed across the ground catching their breath, to gather around him. A blessed silence enveloped the zawiya, filling it with an aura of sacred adoration, and the leader of the circle cleared his throat to speak, his voice melodious: "Recite this prayer, and do not teach it to the foolish. This is the commandment of the Prophet Idris, the secret of the names, for the pious wasil. Call upon the prophet as you enter into the vast courtyard of the Rock, the ladder to heaven: 'O possessor of majesty and honor, possessor of bounty, there is no god but you. Supporter of refugees, neighbor to asylum-seekers, friend to the frightened, I beseech you, if, in the foundations of my faith, I was wretched, render me blessed. And if, in those foundations, I was lacking or miserly, render me steadfast with you and righteously guided.'"

The prayer brought me a sense of peace and calm. Isn't God the supporter of refugees, Murad?

Since we're putting it all out there, I can tell you why Sheikh Morsi invited me to that zawiya; he wanted to shore up my spirit and then nail it to one of Jerusalem's walls . . . It was meant to discourage me from writing my novel.

He was worried. He stopped in just now to say goodbye and gave in without a fight when I told him not to come to the station with me tomorrow. I'll board the bus heading to the Marj Ibn Amer kibbutzim by myself.

I told him to wait for me here, at home, until I came back triumphant with my novel. I wanted him to be strong in this last meeting before I left, and I promised to shoot him a quick call or text from time to time, to let him know everything's okay.

He gave me a big hug. "Nur, my friend, are you really too stubborn to break this promise to yourself about Magdalene? If you want to learn about the landscape around Megiddo and the ruins of Al-Lajjun, why can't you do it online? Watch some videos. Forget this adventure, brother . . . "

He shook his head. "The kibbutz isn't Jerusalem or Tel Aviv; it's a settlement—a military outpost—and it's their first line of defense. Wipe Or's features off your face, come back to yourself, and drop this—it's crazy . . . And no, don't get mad; I'm just nervous for you . . . I know you're ready for what comes next, and I know your cover story is solid—but I wish you'd let sleeping dogs lie . . . "

I didn't respond, just kissed his forehead and thanked him for his kindness and generosity. If he hadn't helped me by forging Or Shapira's ID, none of this would've happened . . . and nor would anything that's yet to come.

Really, what would I have done without him? He's the one who took me in and looked after me for five years. He's not so different from us . . . he's a refugee, too. Maybe that's what pushed him to take care of me. He's a refugee displaced from his first home in the Moroccan Quarter, which was transformed by bulldozers into the plaza facing the Buraq Wall, which became known as the Wailing Wall over Solomon's temple in the wake of the '67 Naksa and the occupation of all Palestine. Morsi's a refugee, but he never put on a mask like I did. Instead, he put on Jerusalem, in all her sacredness, her alleys and side streets, her history, her layers of time.

Jerusalem . . . my beloved and the cornerstone of my redemption. Jerusalem, where every time, every era, bears a kiss of the holy, and whose holiness draws time to itself in pilgrimage.

Yes, Murad . . . There are different ages and times in this homeland exhausted by the Nakba and all the calamities that followed. Sheikh Morsi has his own time, a sacred one, to spend in the halls of his Sufi zawiya, steadfast in his devotion, cursing the fates around him as they wait to pounce, seeking to take refuge in him and settle there. The camp has a time, its ticking hands the stagnant alleyways and my father's silence, and Ramallah has a time, one that cut my father's short. The settlement atop Jabal al-Tawil in Al-Bireh, which my father fought against, has its time. Occupation checkpoints have their own time, one that stages a constant assault on ours. Tel Aviv, Mishmar HaEmek, the Albright Institute: all have their own times. As do Ayala Sharabi and Brian Moore, Emily and Nicole. Even in detention, you have a time of your own . . . But me, I don't have time—there's no time for me . . . because now I feel as though I'm headed at a breakneck speed toward some unknown . . . Does the abyss have its own time?

Murad . . . I've been so eager to talk with you lately, to tell you everything. Did you know that there's a difference between narrating a story and writing it? Of course you did . . . Narration is speech, and writing is words on paper. But there's another massive difference . . . Scheherazade, Murad. Narration is *life* . . . I talk to you so that I can live, like Scheherazade, who withstood more than a thousand nights with her executioner, Shahryar, facing him down with her stories. The story's the Holy Grail . . . And I will tell it, my friend.

I'll keep talking with you as long as my phone still has storage space for my groans and confessions.

Only the dead have the right to talk, and the living dead are all around me . . . Zombies . . . Zombie corpses bloated with pestilence, rot, and impotence . . . I'm suffocating, Murad—save me.

* * *

"God, you're exhausting . . . Don't you want to get some sleep before you leave?"

Silence.

"Are you really not going to answer? I'm so sick of you . . ."

"What do you want?"

"To talk."

"*Now* you acknowledge me. After I snuck into your head . . ."

"No, you impersonated me . . . You don't know anything about me, actually—just the info on my ID and the photo you replaced with yours. You know nothing. You don't know if I'm married, what I do for work, what I like, what I hate, what my hobbies are. Do I smoke? Drink? What's my favorite sex position? Where am I now? You don't know a thing, you numbskull . . . You made stuff up and slapped labels on me that never actually fit."

"Why would I need all that crap? It's enough to know what advantages you have, what you look like, your incredibly Ashkenazi Zionist name. I want the rights you contrived here: your right to exist and move freely, to settle and occupy, to make arrests and assassinate people, your right to displace me, confiscate my property, exclude and marginalize me . . . I want to learn all the Zionist names for things so I can stand up to you."

"You're a bitter, spiteful man. Chill. I've never killed a

Palestinian in my life. Fine, I did serve in the army—in a select unit, like she guessed. Ayala."

"So you didn't have the chance to kill someone."

"Yes . . . No . . . Listen, I never killed any of you, believe me."

"What's the point?"

"What's the point of you knowing what my life looks like? Aren't you busy writing a novel about Mary the Adulteress? What have I got to do with that? Why are you dragging me into the labyrinths of history with you? Is that how you're planning to get revenge on me now?"

"I'm not as spiteful as you think, and Magdalene wasn't an adulteress, you idiot. Taking your identity will give me everything I need because it'll give me access to information and the chance to move freely in the country you stripped us of. I want to understand you so I don't become *like* you. I want to use you to free myself from you."

"Now I'm just confused . . . How are you planning to free yourself from me if you're impersonating me?"

"I told you, I'm not impersonating you. I'm understanding you. I'm learning you . . . I want to know how you see reality."

"And what have you found out so far, genius?"

"I found myself, reflected in your mirror."

"And what does that mean?"

"I was born from you . . . from Zionism and the Nakba you inflicted on me. I'm a part of you, and you're a part of me."

"Bullshit."

"It's true. And once I learn you, I'll be able to separate myself from you, and you can do the same."

"For God's sake. How?"

"The secret lies hidden in the mirror. The mirror's the equation and all its components . . . it's two beings, one controlling and the other subservient. You're Or, in control, and I'm Nur, the subservient. That's why I have to smash the mirror."

"You couldn't smash an ant."

"You'll feel it once you stop being able to make out your own features in the mirror. You won't see your face anymore . . . The face you see will be radiantly human."

* * *

[MONDAY, APRIL 26 – DAWN, JERUSALEM: MARY MAGDALENE AND PETER]

Reading the Gnostic texts and gospels makes me want to learn more about the relationship between Peter, as one leader of the early church, and Mary Magdalene, as another.

I'm looking at their quest to legitimize their respective discourses: the masculine Petrine doctrinal discourse and Magdalene's feminine mystical discourse. A passage in the Secret Gospel of Thomas, cited by Riane Eisler in her book *The Chalice and the Blade*, confirms the extent of Peter's persecution of Magdalene:

> "Simon Peter said to them (the disciples): 'Let Mary leave us, for women are not worthy of Life.' Jesus said, 'I myself shall lead her, in order to make her male, so that she too may become a living spirit, resembling you males. For every woman who will make herself male will enter the Kingdom of Heaven.'"

"Male," in this case, referred to the complete human being, the enlightened union of male and female, and that's what Peter was rejecting.

When I look at the historical context after Jesus's crucifixion, it's obvious that the disappearance, or exclusion, of Magdalene from the gospels is to some extent linked to Peter's post-crucifixion call to choose an apostle to replace Judas Iscariot, who betrayed Jesus to the Jews (Matthias—see Acts 1:15-26). In this important step, Peter declared himself the first head of the Church and thus the only one with the key to Christian law and doctrine; this allowed him to eliminate, once and for all, his strongest competitor: Magdalene.

That's how the masculine approach won out over the feminine and Magdalene's mystical presence disappeared from official Biblical texts. Which leads to multiple questions about Magdalene herself, including how old she was when she first believed in Jesus, whether she was married, and when and where she died.

PS: Murad, today's the day I leave for Kibbutz Mishmar HaEmek . . .

I still haven't slept, but I do need rest, especially after yesterday, which was so eventful it nearly cost me my alter ego. Things got off to a bad start when Ayala Sharabi cornered me in the institute's lab. She said she'd spotted me that morning coming out of Herod's Gate and that I should be careful. She was just trying to warn me how serious the situation was, and how I might get attacked by Arab agitators or provocateurs because things were rough right now. She said it just like that, all alarmed. No difficulty whatsoever uttering such a dehumanizing sentence . . . So. How did I respond?

Well, I got awkward . . . I felt like I'd fallen into the trap of Or Shapira's gloating over me . . . I stared at her for a few moments and then said, "Al-Quds—I mean, Yerushalayim—is quiet in the morning, so I decided to take a walk through the Old City from Jaffa Gate, to enjoy the warmth of our golden city. Did you forget the Temple Mount is ours, Ayala? Remember that whole military declaration when we won the Six-Day War in '67, the Arabs' Naksa?"

Is that how Or would've answered in my shoes?

But then she cornered me again, with a religious question

this time . . . She was surprised I was such a Zionist nationalist when I disrespected my religion by not observing the Sabbath . . . "So you're secular, right?" she asked. "What a shocker—Ashkenazi and secular . . . This really is the era of Tel Aviv. Your very own city-state . . . "

Then she burst out laughing in my face, her full breasts quivering with mirth.

I broke away from her to join Nicole and Emily, who were nearly finished assembling the skeleton.

Oh. I forgot to tell you, Murad . . . the skeleton turned out to be a Mongol soldier. He was either killed or severely wounded in the battle of Ain Jalut, which took place between the Mamluk and Mongol armies more than eight hundred years ago on the outskirts of the Marj Ibn Amer plain. They found the skeleton in a rocky cavity on one of the Gilboa Mountain peaks near Beisan. The funny thing is that the cavity was actually a burial chamber, dating back to the Late Bronze Age, so the Mongol soldier (whom I've obviously called Hulegu after the great conqueror) chose to spend his final moments of war in an ancient Canaanite grave.

As for how we figured out the skeleton's ethnic origin, it was through a dental exam; Mongols can be distinguished from other human beings by their shovel-shaped incisors. This ultimately led to a solemn celebration with a very warm and deep embrace between Emily and Nicole, which excited me a little.

Murad . . .

I feel like you're about to vomit on me right now because of all the trivial details I'm heaping on you. Like you're going to come after me, yelling, "You're a nobody . . . You're not my friend Nur . . . you're lost . . . some demon has taken over your body and left you crazy and confused . . . " Well, you might be right. This is what I was trying to get ahead of by preserving my inner Nur. Didn't I tell you? I'm two people now: Nur and Or.

Anyway . . . Yesterday afternoon, after a day volunteering at the institute with Ayala the Zionist breathing down my neck, I was about to go to Sheikh Jarrah to express my solidarity with the residents against the settlers attacking their homes. I was going to join the activists, supporters, and protestors—local and foreign—who are there. But then I thought, *Wait . . . who am I going as: Nur or Or?* I mean, if the motive is solidarity . . .

Just imagine! Have we really sunk so low, Murad? We're "showing solidarity" with each other now? Who ever heard of a group dividing itself up like that—half of us worried about showing solidarity while the other half suffers under occupation? Like all we are is guest stars in the struggle.

Didn't you tell me the struggle brings people together? Well, they're rising up, united across sector and class in the struggle against the colonizer . . . On the last Nakba Day, they—or some of them, or the remnants of them—showed solidarity by releasing over seventy black balloons into the skies around Ramallah and its refugee camps.

You're a refugee and a prisoner—didn't any of those balloons make it to you?

Oh, right . . . sorry, I forgot there's no sky in prison.

At any rate, my friend . . . When I asked myself which persona I would use to express my solidarity, I backed down, choosing to make do with the room, the institute, and the road between them till this afternoon, when I'll head to Kibbutz Mishmar HaEmek. Because if I showed up as a Palestinian Arab, as myself, they would insult me, beat the shit out of me—obviously—and then arrest me, throwing me out of Jerusalem altogether. And if I showed up as Or, wearing his mask, I would be violently attacked by extremist settlers calling me a traitor and an enemy of the Jewish state and its holy book. They would curse me and yell about how I was a leftist, and anti-Israel, how I hated the God of Israel. And that, in turn, would draw attention to me. Everyone around me—activists, settlers, journalists, police, border guards, and the tortured and displaced residents of Sheikh Jarrah—might all get together to ask me a single question: "Who, for God's sake, are you?"

So now I'm back in my stone room in Silsila. I just executed a brilliant retreat from Ayala without her noticing, ignoring her resentment over my continued refusal to accept a ride home, to the spot where Or is supposed to be living on Jaffa Street, a long way away from his "real" home in Tel Aviv . . .

I came back here for my last evening in Jerusalem, my friend, myself again for a moment inside this ancient house, surrounded by the warmth of the family that has embraced me, its fatherhood, motherhood, brotherhood. I sought refuge in Or, too, and the last dance I would soon sketch out at Kibbutz Mishmar HaEmek on the Plain of Armageddon. But, hang on—should I be using the term "settlement" to refer to Mishmar HaEmek, or "kibbutz"?

Okay . . . Don't get annoyed . . . You're the one who got me obsessed with the language of colonialism . . . no?!

Part III

Sama'

... [Mary Magdalene] said [to the disciples],
"I saw the master in a vision and I said to
him, 'Master, today I saw you in a vision.'
He answered and said to me, 'Blessings on
you, since you did not waver at the sight of
me. For where the mind is, the treasure is.'"
—The Gospel of Mary 17-19

T he bus pulled back onto the road, leaving behind a tall man whose bulky backpack made him look even bigger. He stood on the shoulder of Highway 66, which separated the expanse of the Marj Ibn Amer plain from a vast forest carpeting a chain of hills that culminated at Mount Carmel, overlooking the sea at Haifa.

He stared at the scene in front of him, across the highway, where barbed wire fencing flanked by a row of lush cypress and eucalyptus trees formed an orderly border. He saw a gate next to a small booth for security personnel and a large sign in Hebrew that read "Kibbutz Mishmar HaEmek."

A shiver ran through him, nearly knocking him to the ground to suffocate beneath his heavy pack as he mentally retreated into the alleyways of his camp, farther away now than ever.

He lingered for a moment before crossing the road, the April afternoon saturated with the warmth of a sun that would soon slip irresistibly into the sea at Haifa. He heard a whisper coming from his bag: Nur al-Shahdi pleading with Or Shapira.

"Or . . . I told you, if you can just be good, this is the last time I'll pretend to be you."

"Oh-ho, are you begging me now? And in a whisper? What happened to all that bravado you were working on?"

"This place scares me . . . It's a big deal; this is the first time I've been to a settlement."

"It's a kibbutz, not a settlement; its roots go deep. Welcome to one of the most important socialist kibbutzim in Israel."

"Are you going to expose me, Or? Tell them I'm Palestinian, and a refugee?"

"I dunno yet, but I get the feeling this is going to be fun. Come on, let's go."

"We're not here to have fun; we're here to work."

"Nope—here for fun!"

He crossed the street, heading toward the metal security booth. A thought occurred to him, and he took his phone from his pocket and sent Ayala a message on the expedition's WhatsApp group, telling her he'd arrived and inviting her to come meet him if she was already there. He made his way toward the huge settlement that sprawled over the edge of the plain and clung to the slopes of a forest-covered mountain. The forest, Mishmar HaEmek, was part of the neighboring Megiddo National Park.

Another shiver ran through him. More intensely this time. He was only a few steps away from the security booth.

"You know what this forest is hiding, Or?"

"No idea. Now shut up so you don't blow our cover before the game even starts."

"The 'game' started seventy-plus years ago, back when your ancestors planted corpses and trees side by side on this mountain. They were covering up what was left of Abu Shusha, the village whose people you displaced and killed during the Nakba in '48."

"Um, no . . . You're just a spiteful asshole with an absurd appetite for historical facts. This forest? My ancestors planted it for recreation: hiking, picnicking, camping—that's it . . . Give it a rest with the death and destruction, or I'll bring all of this down around your ears right now."

His phone pinged: a message from Ayala saying that she'd already gotten there and was on her way to the gate to meet him. Then he reached the booth. There was a man inside who seemed to be at the ready, alert and periodically scrutinizing the camera feeds, his tall, muscular frame like a coiled spring. He turned his attention to Or, whose features were not unlike his own.

Or quickly addressed him in his confident Ashkenazi Hebrew. "Hello! I'm Or Shapira. I'm here for the dig."

The security guard responded evenly: "Welcome. I'm Natan Khodrovsky, the kibbutz security officer." He sat back down at his small desk and began searching his computer for the list of names for the expedition, to be sure Or's was on it. He scrolled for a few moments, then said, "Yes, you're on the list, but I'll need to see some ID . . . national ID card, driver's license, passport . . . "

This time, it was Nur's heart that stopped, not Or's. He pulled himself together as he handed the ID to Natan, whose straightforward demeanor suggested to Or that he was dead serious about his role in keeping the kibbutz safe. And despite the golden Star of David necklace that Or wore to prove his Jewishness, Natan narrowed his eyes as he examined the ID; the narrower they got, the more of an expert he seemed, and the more Nur—terrified of being discovered—panicked. But he'd trained for this moment, so he pretended with every fiber of his being to be calm and composed, and managed to pull it off. As Natan stood up again to tell Or everything was in order, he heard the sound of a car horn coming from inside the kibbutz. It was Ayala in her silver Mazda, sticking her head out of the window and shouting happily as she parked next to the booth, "Or's one of us, Natan! Blue and white, all the way!"

Natan laughed, and Nur and Or laughed together. Then Natan handed him back his blue ID, looking serious, and Nur's laughter faded a little when he said, "Mr. Shapira, you need to renew your ID. Didn't you know it should be replaced with a plastic card?"

"Of course! Yeah, I know . . . Working with ancient artifacts just kind of leaves you detached from modern life." He grinned Or's confident Ashkenazi smile, shook Natan's hand, and headed toward Ayala's car. He put the bag in the back of the car, then sat down next to Ayala, who was beaming, pleased that Or Shapira had deigned to swallow his Ashkenazi arrogance and ask for a ride into the settlement, not knowing, of course, that she was just a cover, providing him safe passage into Natan's kibbutz with all its Zionist security measures.

She drove slowly, taking a right, away from the settlement's vital infrastructure and workshops. On the righthand side, Nur spotted a monument that had been partially damaged; Ayala noticed him staring and responded to his surprise at its appearance with pride: "It's called Pinat Hagola, the Corner of the Diaspora; it's a memorial to the Jewish kids who died in Nazi extermination camps during World War II. The damage is from a shell that hit it during the Battle of Mishmar HaEmek against the Arabs, during the 1948 War of Independence."

Or didn't comment. Nur was confused, feeling that he hadn't quite gotten a hold on himself yet. He was right. He was now making his way deeper into the settlement than he had into Jerusalem, just like Sheikh Morsi had warned him.

He almost caved and begged Ayala to take him back, to rescue him from the horrors he was about to plunge into headfirst.

She broke through his confusion as they pulled up to the expedition headquarters: "Everybody's already here . . . Some of them came yesterday, but most people got here this morning . . . Did you know there are no Jews here except you and me?"

"Really?"

"Yeah . . . So you'll have to take good care of me here."

He responded playfully. "Ayala, we're on a noble old Zionist kibbutz; the people who live here are masters of the land . . . we're not on some university campus in Rome or Berlin. Don't worry."

"If you say so . . . Okay, we're here! Brian will get you set up."

She left him and his bag in front of the dig headquarters and went to park her car in the nearby lot.

Or stood in front of a large, rectangular building two stories tall. Its architectural style was reminiscent of an army barracks, the number of windows indicating the presence of many rooms inside. Next to the huge building were smaller, rectangular annexes of a single story, as well as a basketball court parallel to the sloping shoulder of the mountain, with its lush forest. He looked around, searching for the settlement's houses and residents and saw a small house surrounded by a flourishing garden about a hundred meters away. He realized that the buildings in front of him were built away from the settlement's residents and their daily activities, and that comforted him a little.

He was jolted from his contemplation when Brian appeared, his presence reviving him. "Hello, Or! Late, as always."

He responded with an American twang to his accent. "But I always get here in the end!"

They shared a quick laugh and shook hands, and then Brian took him into the building. Inside, the stillness was palpable, pervading the lobby, to the right of which was the conference room and, to the left, the dining hall, in addition to a corridor leading to some dorm rooms and offices and a staircase leading to the second floor. A small number of dig participants, both men and women, were sitting on the couches, absorbed in their cell phones and laptops.

Brian sensed Or's bewilderment and said, "You seem tired from your trip . . . You got here late, so I can tell you we already assigned rooms. The first expedition meeting is at seven; we'll have introductions and form work teams then, and we'll do a quick overview of what was accomplished in the first dig season."

"Great."

Handing him a key to one of the rooms, Brian added, "It's your luck that's great; you get this room all to yourself!

Unfortunately, your roommate came down with corona and couldn't leave France. Come on, let me show you where it is."

They left the main building and walked a few steps before turning right toward a one-story building with just a handful of rooms, built into the mountainside and looking out at the forest. They pushed open the door and went down a long hallway that separated two rows of rooms. Brian stopped and pointed, saying politely, "Your room's the last one on the left. See you at seven!"

Brian hadn't told him who was staying in the rooms around him, which irritated him slightly despite his sigh of relief, a burning exhale that escaped his chest when he realized he'd gotten past his first hurdle: entering the settlement.

He closed the door to his room and looked around. A small room, no more than twenty square meters, with a single window that looked out at the trees, in addition to a bathroom with a big rectangular mirror and a toilet. For furniture, it contained a small wooden desk with a plastic chair across from a metal bunk bed, as well as a wardrobe for clothes and other odds and ends.

He threw his bag on the floor and collapsed onto the bed with another sigh, his chest still tingling with the thrill of adventure.

His watch said it was five o'clock, which gave him two hours to get ready for the next phase, which would be teeming with members of the expedition. He decided to organize his things, dividing them between the wardrobe and the desk, then take a shower to rinse off the worries of travel and clear his mind to record a new voice memo. He would outline his most recent concepts and suppositions about Magdalene in a whisper. Time echoed noisily now in English and Hebrew, while his own time, his private moments in Arabic, were furtive, shrouded in utmost secrecy.

[MONDAY, APRIL 26, EVENING: GNOSTIC MARRIAGE]

About Magdalene's gospel. Boulos Feghali's book *The Gnostic Movement: Its Ideas and Documents* gives us a clear picture that includes excerpts from Gnostic literature, the most important of which are from the Magdalene gospel, estimated to have been written in either Palestine or Egypt in the late first century AD.

The gospel begins with the phrase "The Gospel according to Mary," and you could say it's pure Gnosticism because it's not focused on the historical story of Jesus the way it's presented in the Synoptic gospels. Instead, it contains two dialogues, one between Jesus and his disciples about faith, light, and truth, the other at a crucial moment after Jesus's crucifixion, when the disciples are grieving and worried. Magdalene shores up their spirits by reciting Jesus's secret teachings and commandments during a meeting that was either on the Mount of Olives or in the upper room where Jesus ate the Last Supper with his disciples.

I won't get into the text's content, obviously, since it's so purely Gnostic; what interests me, instead, is analyzing Mary Magdalene's place among the disciples when she tells them, " . . . let us praise his greatness, for he has prepared us and made us truly human."

According to the Gnostic interpretation, what she means by "human" is the divine mind, which is made up of both male and female, and is the origin of light and all beings. Some of the disciples knew that Jesus had favored Magdalene, which is why Peter was forced to speak to her:

> Peter said to Mary, "Sister, we know the savior loved you more than any other woman. Tell us the words of the savior that you remember, which you know but we do not, because we have not heard them."

Mary answered and said, "What is hidden from you I shall reveal to you."

Then she gives this speech where she tells them about Jesus revealing himself to her in a Gnostic vision, and she tells them what he taught her. She finishes recounting the vision and sighs, and *then* comes the drama, the event that will herald Magdalene's exclusion and her persecution by Peter and some of the other disciples:

> Andrew answered and said to the brothers, "Say what you think about what she said, but I do not believe the savior said this. These teachings certainly are strange ideas."
>
> Peter voiced similar concerns. He asked the others about the savior: "Did he really speak with a woman in private, without our knowledge? Should we all turn and listen to her? Did he prefer her to us?"
>
> Then Mary wept and said to Peter, "My brother Peter, what do you think? Do you think that I made this up by myself or that I am lying about the savior?"
>
> Levi answered and said to Peter, "Peter, you always are angry. Now I see you arguing against this woman like an adversary. If the savior made her worthy, who are you to reject her? Surely the savior knows her well. That is why he has loved her more than us.
>
> "So, we should be ashamed and put on perfect humanity and acquire it, as he commanded us, and preach the good news, not making any rule or law other than what the savior indicated."

It's clear at this point that the believer's "perfect humanity" is the result of the mystical and Gnostic marriage between male and female . . . between Jesus and Mary Magdalene.

PS: Can you hear me, Murad? I'm sorry about the

whispering—I'm in the heart of the kibbutz now. The settlement, I mean . . . I know you think the word "kibbutz" whitewashes the colonial nature of Zionism, so I won't call it that. You and your constant analysis . . . So, okay, it's a settlement. Settlement, settlement, settlement. When you talk about names and details, this is what you mean, isn't it?

Anyway, here I am, in yet another room . . . It feels like my whole life has been a series of rooms. A room in the camp . . . in Jerusalem . . . in this settlement . . . But let me give you the good news: I breached the first wall of Zionist defenses, Or Shapira be damned! Natan Khodrovsky (the security guard) and Ayala Sharabi, too.

And actually, let me make a note here; I think it's important . . . When we entered the settlement, I caught a glimpse of a memorial to child victims of the Holocaust. It was a little bit damaged, and Ayala told me it got hit by a shell during the Battle of Mishmar HaEmek, between the Arab Liberation Army and Zionist militias during the Nakba. What caught my attention from her spiel was that the famous Zionist sculptor Zeev Ben-Zvi refused to restore the monument after the fighting, even though it was the Zionists' first Holocaust memorial site in Palestine. My thought was, look how well they succeeded in incorporating the Holocaust here. They went so far as to make it a foundational event—from 1948 till today. Was the Holocaust the catalyst for the Zionist state? Does one tragedy create another?

Because the real Holocaust memorial, my friend, is the Nakba itself. At least, that's what these trees around me bear witness to; they're the headstones of forgotten graves for the victims from the devastated village of Abu Shusha.

* * *

When he entered the conference room, sharp in his resolve, mask firmly in place, Ayala pulled him toward her in the pandemonium, the loud noises interspersed with whispers, smiles, and laughter from fifty or more attendees of diverse backgrounds: researchers, supervisors, hobbyists, volunteers, students, and recent university graduates. Most of them were from abroad, and they varied in age, the oldest over seventy and the youngest in his early twenties. Among them was Ayala, who led him by the hand to a row of seats at the back of the room overlooking the podium. She reproached him teasingly in her Sephardic accent: "Where did you disappear to, you trouble-maker? It's only day one!"

"I was unpacking, and then I rested for a bit."

"Who's your roommate?"

"I don't have one."

"What?! That's your Ashkenazi luck for you! I got stuck with two roommates: the Belgians, Emily and Nicole."

Or leaned toward her, a sly glint in his eye, and whispered, "Better be careful; I hear they're lesbians . . . "

They laughed, stopping when Brian stepped up to the podium and picked up the microphone to begin their kickoff meeting, cutting short the murmur of conversation by clearing his throat.

"Good evening, everyone."

The attendees responded to him in a low chorus, and he continued: "Time to get to work! Let's have some quick introductions, and then we'll get into the theoretical and practical details of the expedition."

What followed was an onslaught of the names, ages, nationalities, and specialties present in the conference room. Most of the expedition members seemed to be from the United States and Canada, with a smaller number from Europe, as represented by the two Belgians, three Poles, five Italians, two British researchers, and a single Swiss man.

"My name's Ayala Sharabi; I'm from here, Israel. I went to the Hebrew University's Institute of Archaeology."

"My name's Or Shapira, from Israel, and I work as a tour guide and archaeologist."

"I'm Sama' Ismail; I'm a graduate student in archaeology from Haifa, from here."

The last voice, husky and feminine, came from his left, just next to him, emanating from a silken-haired woman wearing all black. It sent a series of shivers down his spine that almost forced him out of the conference room. Nur al-Shahdi all but fainted as the Palestinian Arab name hit him, hard: Sama' Ismail from Haifa, the letters *Ha* and *'ayn* landing cool and tranquil on his ear. Sama'—sky. He turned toward her sharply upon hearing such a radiant name and quivered slightly—he couldn't pretend otherwise—then regained his composure to focus on the remaining names of the expedition members. Ayala noticed the quiver and asked him in a whisper if he was okay. He told her he was just tired; he hadn't slept well the night before. As for the young woman to his left, what could he say to her now? What could he say to Sama' when he'd already given her a name that wasn't his to give and a lineage that denied his own roots—when the warmth of his breath left her cold?

He pulled himself together and straightened his mask in silence, sitting next to a woman whose face he still hadn't glimpsed properly but which glittered like a Haifa beach, maskless. He struggled to concentrate on what Brian was saying about the expedition and its objectives, opening his remarks by thanking the Albright Institute and the Israel Antiquities Authority, as well as the Kibbutz Mishmar HaEmek board of trustees, for their generous sponsorship of the expedition. Brian then introduced the primary supervisors, in addition to Dr. Rotem Revivo, the inspector from the Antiquities Authority. He announced that they would need to divvy up into four equal teams, each with ten members and a supervisor presiding over their research and the square of earth they were excavating. He left it up to them to form the teams but emphasized the importance of basic health precautions due to COVID.

Ayala leaned toward Or and asked in a whisper if she could join his team; she didn't speak English as well as he did, and having him nearby would save her the trouble of constantly translating her thoughts for the others. Or shrugged, acquiescing. Nur, meanwhile, tried desperately to calm his racing heart, which was demanding that he join Sama' Ismail's team. Luck wasn't on Nur's side this time, though; she chose a team that was mostly Americans and Canadians.

Ayala chose his team for him as he sat there dumbly, unable to come up with any objections. Emily and Nicole would be joining them, as well as Tony and John, the two American specialists he'd met at the Albright Institute; a Swiss guy; an elderly British man; and two Canadians, all of whom he would soon meet properly over dinner in the dining hall, where they would have a chance to get to know each other better. Once the four teams were established, Brian introduced Professor Peter Henderson, his colleague at Harvard and a co-supervisor of the expedition, to address the research hypothesis behind the excavation. Clicking through a series of close-up photos on the overhead projector, the professor explained the nature of the Roman Sixth Legion site. The sixty-something, who had the silver beard of an academic and a melodious, engaging voice, outlined the biggest findings from the first excavation season and the objectives of the second. But Nur might as well have been in another room; Sama' was sitting to his left, and he was lost in his thoughts. Was she the only Palestinian Arab in this settlement, or was he there, too?

The question cut deep, wounding him and leaving him even more confused and absent as Or seized the opportunity to whisper in his ear, "You lucky devil! An Arab girl on your left and a Jewish one on your right."

"Oh, shut up . . . I'm warning you—keep her name out of your mouth."

"How chivalrous of you. Chill . . . Or have you already forgotten what you did to Ayala in those fantasies of yours?"

"I told you—shut up, or I'll lose it completely; then we'd both be free of this shitty game."

"Oh, we're just getting started . . .! Patience, my friend, patience. So tell me, how is it you're planning to enchant this beautiful Arab? Gonna breathe sweet nothings into her ear? Which language will you use—mine or yours?"

Ayala nudged him on the shoulder, bringing him back to himself and signaling the end of the session. It was time for them to join their team. He turned sharply to his left, but Sama' was gone; she'd disappeared. Ayala noticed his confusion. "What's wrong? Something's up with you."

"I'm a little tired . . . sorry . . . please apologize to the team for me. I'm going to my room to rest a bit. I'll see you guys in the morning."

"And the schedule?"

"Send it to me on WhatsApp."

Then he slipped out of the conference room, leaving Ayala dumbfounded by his apparent mental disarray. Without turning his head, he feverishly scanned every corner of the room for Sama' until he found her sitting with her team, addressing them animatedly. She was too far away for him to make out her features, and he went back to his room dejected.

* * *

[MONDAY, APRIL 26, JUST BEFORE MIDNIGHT:
THE ROMAN SIXTH LEGION]

It's important for me to be familiar with the background of my novel—the Roman Sixth "Ironclad" Legion's camp—so I can map out the space for my protagonist, Naseem Shakr. From there, I need to strengthen the links between Magdalene's secret follower, Simon the Lame; the secret box he passed down to his grandson, Misk al-Attar; and the legion's location just south of the Tel Megiddo archaeological site . . . The site doesn't interest me as much as the depopulated village of Al-Lajjun, which is adjacent to it in the west and on whose ruins stand a kibbutz— settlement—called Megiddo and some dense forests. I have to figure out how to sneak into the village ruins without looking suspicious . . .

Historically speaking, after putting down the Bar Kokhba Revolt, which was from 132 to 136 AD, the Roman Emperor Hadrian ordered his military commanders to summon the Sixth Legion from Britain and Europe and station it in the north of the country near the Plain of Megiddo. They were tasked with suppressing the remaining pockets of revolt, controlling imperial roadways, and securing the roads leading to Galilee. The legion and the camp had a number of slaves and locals whose job was to serve the soldiers and provide for their needs, which led to the emergence of a community called Legio, after the Roman word for "legion." When the Roman armies, and the Sixth Legion in particular, withdrew from the area in the third century, Legio became a city and was known by the name Massimiano or Massimianopolis throughout the Byzantine era; in the Arabo-Islamic era, its name became Al-Lajjun.

The name Massimianopolis is the thing pushing me to validate the hypothesis that Simon the Lame's family was linked to the material and spiritual legacy of Magdalene . . . The name is related to the word "Messiah," meaning "Christ" or "Savior" in Syriac. This confers a certain sacredness on both Jesus and Mary Magdalene, whom I imagine in the novel ordering that her remains be buried in this location, along with the locks of her hair, her perfume, and her gospel, until the Messiah, Jesus the Savior, came on Judgment Day to raise her from the dead.

Back in the spring of 2018, several specialists in the Roman era were able to determine the exact location of the Sixth Legion using aerial photos and satellite images indicating that south of the Tel Megiddo dig site was a rectangular building surrounded by subterranean depressions. The first excavation work began with the support of the Israel Antiquities Authority, whose team discovered earthen defensive trenches beside the foundations of a large, six-meter-wide wall. Inside the building, the team uncovered rooms likely dating back to one of the camp's barracks; they contained broken roof tiles that bore the insignia of the Sixth Legion, in addition to coins, the rusted remains of shields, and a whole bunch of potsherds. Most importantly, they were able to map out the boundaries of the camp, which spanned 300 meters in width and 500 in length. It was inhabited by more than 5,000 Roman soldiers and a number of slaves and locals.

All of this aside, I still have some misgivings, and I'm not sure yet how valid they are. Like, what's the point of holding such an in-depth second excavation season here? Most of the camp's landmarks have already been discovered . . .

So the Albright Institute and the Israel Antiquities Authority . . . what exactly are they digging for?

PS: Murad, it was really bad. I'm not whispering anymore; I'm in mourning after that woman caught me hiding behind my mask . . . She was next to me, flaunting her true face in all its glory, and miserable refugee that I am, I had the gall to sit there covering my face with someone else's, one that was responsible for my own pain. So now what . . .? Tell me!

She introduced herself as "Sama' Ismail from Haifa, from here."

Not "from Israel." She didn't say she was an Arab Israeli and that she had an Israeli ID . . . Actually, I think I heard Ayala grumbling about that on my right. I did, yeah . . . Ayala complained about the way Sama' introduced herself: "'Here'? Where is 'here'? Call it by its name: Israel. It's the land of Israel, and you're a citizen of it."

Is that true, Murad? Is Sama' Ismail a citizen of the state of Israel, a resident, a guest, or just passing through? Don't citizens need a homeland?

This woman, Sama'—her homeland is Haifa, at least for now.

I know you're about to pounce; I can practically hear you now: *So why didn't you set Ayala straight? And why didn't you shock Sama' by speaking the language you both love so much? Just a few words in Arabic, man, to chase away the coldness . . . a little warmth from the Arabic alphabet!*

You're right . . . But I'm here for a very specific reason: to do historical research for my novel on Magdalene. I don't want to get bogged down by some heated argument that could blow my cover. I don't know what to do . . . How am I supposed to act around her tomorrow? How can I even *be* around her? What language do I use to say good morning?

He stopped recording and sent a short text message to Sheikh Morsi, letting him know he'd made it safely to the expedition HQ and that everyone believed him . . . at least for now. Then he examined the next day's schedule, which Ayala had sent him via WhatsApp, grimacing at the early departure time for the dig site, just five kilometers south of Mishmar HaEmek.

Then he fell into the abyss of sleep, in need of some rest before a day promising both earth and sky.

* * *

CHAPTER 6

A hill overlooking a plain . . .
A knoll carrying twenty cities in its womb, twisting in the pangs of childbirth for thousands of years.

Megiddo,

Woman of the ancient secret,

How many battles have taken place on the smooth bed of your plain, not so smooth for those between the heavens and earth?

How many caravans weighed down with destinies have passed through here?

How many deaths, the dead laid to rest on biers of conspiracy and cunning?

How many emperors have walked here, to their end or to their glory?

How many caliphs have cinched their horses' saddles on the way to the throne or to a poisoned grave?

Bloody Megiddo at the foot of Mount Carmel, the greatest battlefield in history since Thutmose III surprised his enemies from its forested folds. From west of Megiddo, he fell upon them in a brilliant maneuver that the British general Edmund Allenby would employ again 3,500 years later during World War I, defeating the last Ottoman armies under Ataturk. After his victory, he was dubbed "the Lord of Armageddon," a reference to the battle at the end of times.

It's Megiddo, teeming with gods, pharaohs, emperors, kings, caliphs, sultans, the Arab Liberation Army, and Zionist militias.

Even Napoleon Bonaparte, when he passed nearby, insisted on climbing its swelling breast, saying to his soldiers, "All the armies of the world could maneuver their forces on this vast plain."

And here it is, the plain, still waiting for its promised absolution and final salvation spun from the terrifying breaths of the Apocalypse of John. For more than a hundred years, archaeological expeditions have been digging deep within it to extract its entrails and prepare the stage for the resurrection and humankind's last battle.

As for his own battle, it had already broken out. It was the Battle of Nur al-Shahdi, who, along with his team, had been immersed since 6 A.M. in their twenty-square-meter excavation unit. He was reunited with his sole passion, caressing the earth, tickling its crust in pursuit of pleasant banter, which would soon bear fruit when the trial pit laid bare the ecstasy of the earth in all its secrets and histories. It wasn't Or in the pit; it was Nur. He was being pushed farther and farther inside not by his keen archaeological sense and hands skilled in extracting the earth's archives, but instead by his desperation to avoid looking at the unit where she was working with her team. Sama' Ismail, the woman who'd reduced him to dust the day before. He'd been ready for every detail and surprise of his adventure except her, a native plant from his homeland, undisguised, its aroma pervading the air around him.

He swooped down on the earth with his large pickaxe. Beside him worked the team members he'd met early that morning before they boarded the bus for the excavation site a few hundred meters southwest of Tel Megiddo.

Accompanied by words of encouragement and an enthusiastic commentary that kept their spirits high, the team worked at everything from taking notes on the different sections of their square to extracting soil from it, along with the potsherds that, alone, were capable of revealing the pit's secrets. The professor supervising the team squatted next to the trial pit, which was no more than a meter deep, as Nur delved farther into it, working to reach the natural layer, which was perhaps a meter and a half down. David Adams, a professor from England in his sixties, had an overheated face as red as a London lord's and wore a khaki hat that matched his crumpled explorer's vest and trousers. He was impressed by Nur's skill and the way he used a pickaxe to dig without causing any damage to the sections of soil. Little did he know that Nur had graduated from an archaeological institute with subpar facilities that bore no comparison to the foreign institutes of the other participants.

David was encouraging, heaping appreciation and admiration on him for his meticulous work. Ayala and the rest of the team members were busy double-sifting the soil they'd dug out of the pit, first dry and then with water.

Nur worked in silence. It was the everlasting covenant he'd made with the earth, that each time he reconnected with it, he would speak to it in his heart, pleading for it to love him and fold him into its embrace, so he could restore its radiance.

To the people around him, he addressed only a handful of words, avoiding discussions that would pull him away from making love to the earth, until it was time for a break, which Brian announced by calling out, "Okay, friends! Time for breakfast."

It was 9 A.M., three hours after they'd begun toiling away on their little test pit.

Or pulled himself out of the hole, which had almost reached the natural layer, already exhausted and cursing the intensive work schedule. He hadn't expected it to be so stringent, starting with a 5:30 A.M. wake-up time to prepare for the bus to the dig site, where work would begin at six and last until nine, followed by a half-hour break for breakfast to reenergize the participants. Then it would be back to work until 11:30, followed by a blink-and-you-miss-it fifteen minutes of rest before they resumed, finishing at 1 P.M., when, worn out, the expedition would take the bus back to Mishmar HaEmek for lunch in the dining hall. After the meal, they got some time off for a shower and a nap, and at 4 P.M., the entire expedition would reconvene in the lab to clean and number the potsherds and other finds from the dig. And that still wasn't all. After the lab work, there were various lectures by specialists planned, lasting until 8 P.M. After that, dinner and then—finally—some welcome shuteye after a grueling day of work.

Such an intensive schedule wouldn't give Nur the time he wanted to devote himself to his novel. Since the early morning, he'd been stealing glances toward the west of the excavation site, to the presumed location of Al-Lajjun, or the city of Massimianopolis, the setting of his book, on whose ruins stood the settlement of Megiddo amidst dense pine and cypress trees. Fertile ground for his imaginings of Magdalene was within reach, just a stone's throw away, but the surveillance cameras he noted around the excavation site and the settlement were enough to frustrate his efforts to go there. The only thing soothing his annoyance over the exhausting schedule was that it would be the weekend soon. Friday and Saturday. Maybe the long break would give him a new spurt of energy and help him refocus on the novel.

The four teams gathered under the large open shelter that had been set up beside the site to host the expedition members' breakfast, its shade providing a pleasant respite from a sun that ranged in intensity from the prime of spring to the sweltering of early summer. Nur stood next to one of the breakfast tables and looked around, searching for her until he spotted her in the distance, dusting herself off. She didn't come toward them to share breakfast but instead headed toward the south-facing edge of the shelter, where she sat on a chair and buried her nose in her cell phone. He felt lost, and Ayala picked up on it and said, in her guttural Hebrew: "Looks like she's fasting. Didn't you know Arabs have a month where they fast? Ramadan?"

"Oh. Yeah, I know."

Ayala had no idea she'd hit him where it hurt, like a dagger to the heart, Nur's heart, though he hadn't tasted the bitterness oozing from his mask until the day before, with Sama' sitting next to him. He swallowed back the bitterness of forgetting Ramadan, consoling himself for the loss of the holy months he'd left in his past.

The time he was operating in at present was Or Shapira's, who now hissed in his ear, "What's wrong with you? You've been out of it since yesterday. This girl making you miss your roots?"

"You know who has me feeling suffocated and 'out of it' right now?"

"Oh, I know . . . Ayala's suffocating me, too. And you won't even let me have her. You and your ridiculous purity."

"Look at her . . . She's fasting . . . totally in the zone."

"Go over there . . . Or at least spill the beans about who you really are on WhatsApp."

"What would be the point?"

Then he forgot about Or for a few minutes and got to work on the light meal provided: boiled eggs and breakfast meat, labaneh and various salads, complemented by fruit juices and accompanied by short conversations among the participants, whom Nur had met without really even seeing them, or, rather, without distinguishing between them. They were foreigners, he repeated to himself, foreigners with foreign features and foreign names. *Like me, with my blond hair and Ashkenazi features.* It was all about faces, the way faces were classified in this little corner of the world: foreigners, Ayala the Sephardic Jew, Or the Ashkenazi, Sama' the Palestinian. He glimpsed Sama's face when she stood up, abandoning her phone to go back to work in the test square, and he inhaled sharply; she was a lush tree from the slopes of Mount Carmel, no older than twenty-five graceful springs, a perfume from Haifa, tall and stirringly slender, her silky black hair braided down her back, her eyes the colour of a dark, noble night. Her face was a lilac-scented moon, mingling with dusk over the bay, her delicate nose a spotlight for two luscious lips. But he wouldn't have the chance to listen, captive, to her voice until later, during the second break.

He went back to the pit and busied himself anew with the womb of a land that had heralded the birth of Roman military history; the renown of the Sixth Legion now lay beneath his feet. He struggled with it, wielding his pickaxe, and after several long, dusty moments, he was confident enough of his victory to announce to Professor David that he'd managed to reach the natural layer unmarred by the historical progression above it. David came down into the pit, examining with expert eyes the sections of soil in the pit wall, which were beginning to reveal their layers. With full confidence in his English, Or commented, "I think the camp layer is the third from the bottom, under the layer of red dirt."

Brian's voice boomed down into the pit, which he was crouching beside: "Nicely done, Or. You've reached the natural layer first—you beat them all to it! What do you think, David?"

"I think Or's right," David replied in his deep voice, still scrutinizing the bands of soil. "The third layer from the bottom might be our target layer. But let's hang on a minute till the test pits in the other squares are finished."

David and Brian's appreciation of his first achievement on the dig put a little swagger into Or's step, as did the admiration and appreciation he got from his team members, not only because he'd gotten to the natural layer in record time but also because Brian rewarded them with an early break—and a long one—for all their hard work as a team. They hurried back into the soothing shade, where David, who was a master storyteller, regaled them with his exploits: archaeological adventures in the Pharaohs' Egypt, Babylonian and Assyrian Iraq, and other countries abounding in the oldest human civilizations, all while affirming the uniqueness of excavating in the "Holy Land," as he called it.

"It's the living, speaking Bible."

Deep down, David's commentary, shot through with the Western view of the country, didn't sit well with Nur. He felt alienated from his land when it was described in such religious terms, mapped out based on the length and breadth of the Old Testament. But he would never dare say so in a conversation with David Adams, especially now that he was basking in the marvels of praise and admiration: Or Shapira, the skilled excavator, his face now glowing with pleasure as he listened to his British instructor. Eventually, the other three teams joined them in the shelter to take a breather, teasing Or and his team enviously and claiming to resent them because their own break would be shorter. Then they spread out on the various seats under the canopy.

Nur looked around, searching for Sama', and spotted her a few steps away, chatting with one of her colleagues. He hurried toward them, pretending to be looking at some equipment on the table beside them. He wanted to hear her voice, the husky voice of Sama' Ismail, who was addressing one of the Canadian students on her team in fluent English: "Mark, just because I live here doesn't mean I'm Israeli or Jewish . . . hardly. There's a huge difference between being Palestinian and being Israeli!"

The blond Canadian student didn't seem able to fathom this difference, and Nur was about to interrupt their conversation to explain to it to him when Or held him back, whispering in his ear, "And who are you gonna be when you butt into this conversation, you idiot? Or or Nur?"

"Oh, shut up and let me settle this, once and for all."

"Settle what?! What are you going to say? 'Sama' means she doesn't recognize Israel's right to exist, even though she has Israeli citizenship'? And what about you? Are you going to tell him, 'Personally, I'm Palestinian, but I like playing with masks, so by night, I'm Nur and, by day, I'm Or'?"

Ayala dragged him out of his inner dialogue with Or, whispering in sharp, annoyed Hebrew: "What's up with this Arab girl? Is she talking shit about Israel to this dumb Canadian?"

He sidestepped her indignation: "I don't know . . . I didn't hear what she said."

He walked away, leaving the shelter and Sama's husky voice, Sama' who had boldly claimed her Arab Palestinian roots in front of all these foreigners, and her right to be here on this land, without fearing anyone's reproach or the wrath of Zionists like Ayala and him—Or and Nur, who now stared together at the western end of the excavation site, at the Megiddo settlement on the horizon. "What do we do?"

"I don't know."

"How do we get to Al-Lajjun?"

"You mean, how do we get to Kibbutz Megiddo?"

"No, Al-Lajjun—it's a whole village buried under your feet. My god, you guys are masters at cleaning crime scenes, aren't you? Just throw a little green on it, some trees . . . wherever there are trees in my country, there was catastrophe."

"So hostile, man! Trees are life. They're renewal."

"They're death. They're tombstones."

* * *

[TUESDAY EVENING – APRIL 27:
ABOUT THE VILLAGE OF MISK AL-ATTAR]

Al-Lajjun
District: Jenin
Population in 1948: 1,280
Date of Occupation: 30 May 1948
Name of Military Operation: Gideon
Military Unit: Fourth Battalion, Golani Brigade

Settlements on Town Lands Pre-1948: None
Settlements on Town Lands Post-1948: Kibbutz Megiddo
The village of Al-Lajjun is located on a slightly elevated hill in the southwestern part of Marj Ibn Amer and is distributed on both banks of the Wadi al-Lajjun stream.

The Crusaders seized power in Al-Lajjun; then Saladin recaptured it in 1187 AD. Arab travelers and geographers mention it in their historical records, calling it a fertile, well-developed town, full of freshwater springs.

In the late nineteenth century, villagers from Umm al-Fahm moved to Al-Lajjun to take advantage of its arable land. What caught my attention is that, to build their homes, some of the residents later used stones from the Tel Megiddo archaeological site, which was excavated by a German expedition in 1903.

In 1931, the population of Al-Lajjun was composed of 829 Muslims, 26 Christians, and 2 Jews, which lends credence to my proposition that some of Simon the Lame's descendants, the family of Misk al-Attar, would still have been there.

As for Al-Lajjun's archaeological heritage, it vanished completely, with no record or excavation, after Zionist settlers bulldozed the land and its ruins to clear it for planting.

One of the main reasons this village was destroyed during the 1948 Nakba is that it was the base for the Arab Liberation Army's attack on the settlement of Mishmar HaEmek, just five kilometers north of the village, where I am now. During the successful Zionist counterattack twelve days after the Battle of Mishmar HaEmek, dozens of villagers were killed, and the rest of the population was displaced.

On another note, I need to study the German excavation work in the area of Tel Megiddo. During the Ottoman period, the Germans launched expeditions and excavation projects all over Palestine. Interestingly, at the height of the Megiddo excavation, the Kaiser's Oriental Society dispatched archaeologists Heinrich Kohl and Carl Watzinger to excavate the ruins of ancient synagogues in Galilee. Excavations at Tel Hum revealed the remains of the Capernaum synagogue where Jesus preached. I'm guessing that the same excavation work was expanded to include the village of Magdala, where Magdalene was from, as the researchers promptly returned to Tel Megiddo to excavate an archaeological layer specific to the Roman era in the first century AD. From there, it might be posited—for the sake of the novel—that they carried out secret excavations of the city of Massimianopolis, currently Al-Lajjun, looking for traces of Magdalene, but when Germany and the Ottoman Empire were defeated in World War I, they ran out of time.

This proposition gives my main character, Naseem Shakr, a parallel plot to the main Magdalene story.

PS: Murad, buddy . . . I'm exhausted at this point, on the verge of falling asleep. I seriously deserve it after the hard work and heat of the day; it was intense and scheduled down to the minute. I was so busy speaking English and Hebrew today that I forgot it was Ramadan, until she reminded me by isolating herself at the edge of the shelter, fasting, suffering from the exertion, hunger, and thirst all at once. Did I envy her? Yes. I did. Did I hate her? A little . . . I hated her at the same time as I was proud of her, this woman who's so unlike me. I wish I were like her!

Anyway, then we all piled into the bus and came back. Ayala sat next to me, worn out from all the work, which gave me a break from her chattering in Hebrew. We devoured our lunch as soon as we got back. Sama' turned in immediately, heading straight for her room because, like I said, she was fasting, and then the rest of us withdrew, too.

I found out that most of my neighbors in the dorm are Americans, but I haven't been mingling with them the way Or Shapira should. I'm tired—or, rather, chronically fed up with conversation, compliments, and jokes. I'm a son of silence; I was born from it—remember?

The important thing is that I took a good, refreshing shower and lay down, and I was immediately out like a light. After my nap, I had the energy I needed for my favorite job: cleaning and numbering the potsherds we pulled out of the test pit. Then I joined a debriefing session led by Professor Brian about what we accomplished today. Finally, it was dinner, where, by the time we got there, Sama' had already broken her fast—which made me feel even crankier. So I hurried back to the privacy of my room to tell you all this in whispered Arabic. To say, Murad—well, that the warm, husky quality of her voice was like a bulldozer, scooping me up and throwing me into the pit I dug at the excavation site before burying me in her radiant Palestinian presence. She didn't need a mask to erupt in the face of that Canadian student who couldn't spell Palestine, let alone recognize it as our homeland, and yet could easily articulate Israel's right to exist, a conversation that made Ayala happy and angry at the same time. Happy because it reaffirmed to her that the West still has what she considers a conscience, that it's in solidarity with her country and the legacy of the Holocaust. Angry because that country still can't silence Sama'. What makes her that angry? Why does she loathe Sama' when she doesn't loathe me? I mean—Or. *He* treats her like she's less than. Why would she be drawn to an upper-class Ashkenazi who persecuted and marginalized her people under this colonial system? What do you think?

Or persecutes Ayala, Ayala persecutes Sama', and Sama' is the one I'm crying out to now.

My dear friend . . .

It got worse. At some point, I heard a repeated metallic clanging echoing from the southwestern edge of the excavation site. There was a voice shouting out "Roll call!" in rusted, faulty Arabic. I flinched when I noticed that Occupation monstrosity, all iron, cement, and high walls, the Megiddo Prison.

Is that how they keep track of you, Murad? Numbers instead of names, stripping you of your humanity morning, noon, and night? They count your bodies, your breaths, your hopes for freedom.

Are those numbers how they knock you out of the saddle of your dreams? Gnawing away at your mornings with the jaws of their metal bars?

Megiddo Prison, Megiddo Forest, Megiddo settlement . . .

It's this insistence on pillaging history, shackling it through violence, oppression, and control.

It's the settlement of Megiddo I'm fixing on now, Murad. Mary Magdalene is there, calling me, waiting . . . But how to get there when the road is booby-trapped with surveillance cameras, thieves of history, barbed wire, and numbers . . . numbers . . .

* * *

Time rushed past, turning the week into a whirlwind of activity. Moments passed him by, fleeting, making little impact, marking a past he would soon be remembering. Flickers of misshapen memories born and raised in the Mishmar HaEmek settlement and at the Roman Sixth Legion excavation site. Then he decided, with sudden determination, not to just live in the moment, but to piggyback on every sign of a future carrying in its folds the novel he wanted to write. To toss Or Shapira's mask into the margins of the moment once and for all. In the hurricane of time, he stared at his features in the mirror and wondered if some trace of Or Shapira would stay in his soul, in his blood, and whether his intended text was worth relinquishing his original shadow and features. Wasn't he sick of this game of masks and the bitter ache he felt every time he passed Sama' in the streets of Or Shapira's time?

In his first week, he'd found himself competing sometimes against Nur and sometimes against Or, only to be beaten during each round by the blades of ambiguity, denial, confusion, and retreat, as well as the fear of being discovered at any moment.

He managed that first week by immersing himself in the dig, excavating the earth and extracting its pottery and its secrets, heedless of his own shattered pieces, which he hoped to one day see someone gather and return to their point of origin.

Absorbed as he was in his work, he was unable to follow through on his aspirations for the novel, which were settled among the ruins of the village of Al-Lajjun, below the heavily guarded and monitored Megiddo settlement. In spite of his well-crafted Ashkenazi mask, he shrank, abject and afraid, from the outskirts of the settlement. Setting off all his alarm bells and exacerbating that fear, every so often—and for ever so briefly—the Israel Antiquities Authority would send its inspector, Rotem Revivo, to monitor the progress being made at the dig site. The moment she alighted there, he would disappear, pretending he needed to relieve himself or make a phone call, then retreating to the far end of the shelter. If he had even a passing chat with her about his fabricated past, she might latch on and ask about his work background. That would all but guarantee that his mask would be ripped off to the soundtrack of Or Shapira's sneering laughter, and then he would be bound and thrown into the prison that stood across from him: Megiddo Prison.

During breaks, he continued to sneak glances at Sama' Ismail. Just looking at her comforted him; he drew his own purity from her, without daring to approach her or join any conversation in which she took the lead.

Time rushed past, hours of excavation, breaks, conversations, lectures, group meals, voice memos, and the reassurances he made to Sheikh Morsi that he was well via quick phone calls and messages. Time rushed past as he spoke to Ayala in Hebrew, fielding her constant anger and indignation at the presence of this Arab woman who never tired of talking politics and identity, and he evaded her grip as she plotted to ruin Sama' in the most Zionist way possible. "Let her say whatever she wants, Ayala, and then we can do whatever we want . . . Don't you believe in democracy?"

"What democracy? What do Arabs have to do with democracy?! You Ashkenazim are always bragging about democracy, liberalism, and respect for other people's opinions, but in real life, you're more tribal than any of us."

«Ayala, chill. She's expressing a position based on her beliefs; you can always counter with the opposite position."

"My only 'position' is that this country is named Israel. I have only one land, but she has more than twenty of them: Jordan, Syria, Iraq, etc. I mean, go to Dubai! It's beautiful. I visited over the holidays. Have you been?"

"No, I haven't had the chance."

He responded testily, surprised by the way she'd taken the reins of the conversation and led him down other paths, her hatred for Sama' leading to her love of Dubai. She hated Sama', even though she'd still never exchanged a single word with her; the most she'd done was throw a few haughty glances her way when she wasn't looking, something Nur only noticed because he was hyper-aware of both Or and Ayala. But Sama' was absorbed in her work and mingled mostly with her team members.

He was getting more and more worried about the mask, which he felt he'd been wearing for eons, so when Ayala and the rest of the team invited him to go with them that weekend to Lake Tiberius, which they called the Sea of Galilee, he claimed he had to work on a study about the Sixth Legion for an American archaeology journal. He holed up in his room on Friday and Saturday; after all, he was the master of rooms, especially this one on the edge of a forest that reached out to him at night, surrounding him with the howling of wolves. As he lay there, far away from his past, his camp, and his name, the eerie howls punctuated his voice memos, which became quicker and more intense.

[WEDNESDAY NIGHT – APRIL 28]

We found some Roman coins at the dig site today. The expedition was thrilled.

PS: Murad . . . Where am I? And my father, where is he? Ayala's been to Dubai, and I haven't . . . Save me!

[THURSDAY AFTERNOON – APRIL 29]

Brian surprised me today by saying that they found the ruins of a Roman camp in Algeria that looked a lot like our Roman Sixth Legion.

PS: Sama' was sad today, Murad. The clear sky of her face was clouded with sorrow and confusion . . . and I didn't know why. How could I?

[FRIDAY EVENING – APRIL 30]

I still haven't found any artifacts at the dig site to confirm that there was a Christian community within the camp walls, so I need to do everything in my power to visit the ruins of Al-Lajjun in the Megiddo settlement.

PS: Murad—the situation in Jerusalem is getting tenser by the day. The settler occupation's attacks on the residents of Sheikh Jarrah are escalating.

. . . did you know I'm all alone in this damn building today?

[Saturday Afternoon – May 1]

The well in Al-Lajjun is calling to me . . . Misk al-Attar's well is luring me into its depths. I need to find it for Naseem Shakr because, without it, he won't be strong enough to write his novel. At this point, I feel like the well I've imagined really exists.

PS: Murad—in my isolation, silence has descended, and it's making me miss my father's silence in the alleyways of the camp. Though I can hear upbeat music coming from houses in the settlement . . . I forgot to tell you—today is Labor Day, and this settlement is socialist and secular. How is that even possible? Isn't socialism meant to create humane conditions, not the conditions of a nakba?

[Sunday, Dawn – May 2]

Today we'll put the finishing touches on our test pit. Fingers crossed for some great surprises.

PS: Murad . . . have I told you what Sama' Ismail's face looks like in the early morning? It looks like Sidrat al-Muntaha, the tree marking the farthest boundary of the seventh heaven. Or, no . . . it looks like Eid morning. The Eid of a long-ago childhood.

[Monday Night – May 3]

Today we found a medium-sized metal box. When I saw it, my heart skipped a beat . . . For a moment, I felt that everything I'd imagined was completely true. The discovery of the box caused quite a commotion, accompanied by clapping, yelling, etc. We opened it, taking every possible precaution, and the rusty spearhead inside dashed our ambitions for the dig. And then—fiasco—the Israel Antiquities Authority inspector Rotem Revivo showed up with Natan the security guard, and I had to go into hiding till they left.

PS: Ayala knocked on my door today, but I wasn't the one who answered. It was Or.

Had Nur al-Shahdi gone mad, or had the torrential flow of a time that wasn't his swept him into the depths of a bottomless abyss?

He'd woken to the sound of his door squeaking. It stood open, which was unusual. He rolled out of bed and put on his mask, hurrying to the door to close it, but it wouldn't close. He stopped in his tracks at the sound of a feral moan coming from the room opposite his and stepped outside, looking right and left before crossing the hall. He pushed open the door, drawn in by the intensity of the moan, and the image came sharply into focus with a hiss of fierce lust. Ayala was pressed between Emily and Nicole, each woman with one of her firm breasts in her mouth, ravenous. Blinded by the gleam of their slim naked bodies, he backed away and collided with a human form, turning toward it with a start. It was Or, wearing nothing but a carnal smirk. Or pushed him forward; he stumbled, almost fell, put his hands to his face to check that the mask was still intact, looked in the mirror. The moans and the sound of bare limbs slapping urgently against each other scorched him. He stared into the mirror but saw only Or. When he turned around, there, too, he found only Or. He shuddered. Or pushed him aside as Nicole and Emily grabbed Ayala's arms and legs and Ayala groaned, "Come on, Or, melt me! Come pound me with that Ashkenazi dick."

He moved toward her, then pressed her down into the bed and penetrated her with everything ecstatic and cruel within him. She wriggled free from Nicole and Emily, who were entangled again, their breath and the friction between their bodies accelerating. Ayala stared up at Nur standing beside the bed, her face and chest flushed, voice strangled by desire, "I need you inside me—hurry!"

Nur yearned toward her, so stirred by her indecency that he almost took off his clothes. He was about to give her what she wanted when he turned, all at once, toward the window and saw Sama' Ismail leaning against the trunk of a towering pine, staring at him sadly for a few moments before suddenly scaling the tree and disappearing into its branches.

* * *

"Sabah al-khair!"
"Sabah al-nur!"
The cheery morning greeting in Arabic wasn't his, despite the intense shiver it sent down his spine, but had been spoken by one of her team members, standing next to him under the shelter. The American student blushed and announced that it was impossible to pronounce the letter *Saad* in "sabah" the way Sama' had taught him. Embarrassed, he swapped it out for the English: "Good morning." The response, in better Arabic, was hers, and she was shocked to hear it echoed by Or, his letter *Ha* full-throated and perfect. The latter realized with a start how much confusion he'd just created for himself on this morning graced by Sama' Ismail, who pulled herself together when she glimpsed the Star of David glinting on his chest. She spoke to him in Hebrew: "You're Shapira, right? They call you Big Axe?"

Then she dashed any hopes he had of becoming less flustered around her by adding a masterfully sarcastic greeting in Hebrew. "Boker tov. Though you replied just now in Arabic, which Ashkenazim don't usually speak fluently . . ."

He stammered. He nearly blurted out Arabic letters at random, trying to relieve himself of the burden of Or, who whispered in his ear, "See, you idiot, you're going to give yourself away. Where the hell did that early-morning Arabic come from?"

He answered her in Hebrew. "Boker or, Sama'."

Her jaw dropped, and she exclaimed, still in Hebrew, "You say my name like an Arab, too . . . What kind of Ashkenazi are you?"

Or whispered again, begging, "Enough, please . . . Come on, don't get me involved with her . . . Get a grip."

He forged ahead, gathering his Ashkenazi presence around himself as the American student slunk away, unable to stomach the guttural language so early in the morning. He shrugged. "A lucky one, I guess; I had no idea . . . But Hebrew and Arabic are both Semitic languages, right?"

"Of course. Though if I said no right now, you'd tell me I was antisemitic."

He frowned. "Let's not talk politics . . . we're here for archaeology."

"Antiquities *are* politics, or didn't you know that? Aren't you the ones who turned the Torah into an archaeological guidebook?"

Or whispered indignantly into Nur's ear, "Okay, that's it, this girl is toxic. Ayala's right. Even though, for some reason, she's totally comfortable talking to you—I mean, to me . . . It's insufferable."

Nur was on the point of slipping away from Sama' and her sharp tongue when Ayala pounced, ready to match her sharpness: "Is there a problem?"

Sama's response was derisive: "The only problem here is you."

The derision caused an explosion: "Don't you ever get sick of repeating all that crap to the foreign students? You're always the victims, and we're always the executioners."

Both Or and Nur floundered as Sama' answered her coldly: "It's not crap. It's fact."

Finally, he intervened, pulling himself together just enough to avoid starting the work day with a quarrel: "Please stop . . . There's no need for pointless political discussions."

Or's tone was sarcastic as he whispered in his ear, "Nice . . . that's exactly what I would say if I were you."

Sama' walked off without a word. Ayala, however, was livid. "Why didn't you defend me in front of her? What's wrong with you? Are you going to let this Arab chick spread her hatred to everybody on the expedition?"

"Calm down; we were just talking." He took her hand and caressed it to placate her, skillfully assuming the role of Or the Ashkenazi Jew, and led her to their team's test square so they could start working.

The expedition was progressing by leaps and bounds in the frenzy of excitement occasioned by recent developments, as the pit soil had revealed its secrets more readily than Brian and his co-supervisor, Peter Henderson, had expected. This promised to allow the four teams longer breaks, reinvigorating them. But several times, when Nur—not Or—turned his head, he noticed Brian, Peter, and David holding whispered conversations in serious voices, and he started to think they were digging for something they didn't want to disclose to the whole expedition, something mysterious that grew and spread in his mind, feeding on Nur's active novelist's imagination, making him question—if only to Or—what was going on: "There's something fishy happening . . . they're looking for something specific."

"You're just obsessed . . . Or did you forget that you're on a dig, and these guys are supervising?"

"Of course not, but my gut's never wrong, and it says they're hiding something."

"I heard Brian's an evangelical. Ayala said he lives on a kibbutz nearby with his Jewish wife."

"Of course. We're standing on the field of the final battle between the forces of good and evil, the Battle of Armageddon."

"And which side are you on? Good or evil?"

"You tell me."

He was brought out of his unsettled reverie by the hubbub of children who'd come with their families to volunteer at the site. That morning, Brian had informed the expedition members that a group of residents from the Jezreel Valley Regional Council kibbutzim would be visiting their dig site as part of a summer camp the council had organized for the children.

The noisy crowd surrounded the four test pits, filling the air with the children's joyful curiosity and their excitement about participating in the excavation. With the help of the camp counselor, Brian divided the children and their families up among the four squares. Or's square was assigned one family consisting of a mother and her three children, who ranged in age from seven to eleven years old. David greeted them cordially, like an English gentleman, as did the rest of the group, especially Or and Ayala because, as Ayala said, this family was white and blue like them. Or gave the children basic tools—a brush, a small pickaxe, and a sieve—and gladly gave them instructions on how to use them. He wasn't sure whether the gladness came from Or or Nur, but true, powerful happiness came moments later, thanks to the shining revelation he'd been wishing for since he'd joined the expedition. It was the children's mother who provoked it, as she introduced her family: "I'm Oshrat Tomer, and these are my children Gilad, Yoni, and Eitan. We live at Kibbutz Megiddo—we're neighbors!"

Or trumpeted in Nur's head: "Hallelujah! Didn't I tell you how lucky you were, you asshole? Here comes your chance now, dancing right up to you! Come on, show me that Ashkenazi eloquence."

"Welcome to the Kibbutz of the Roman Sixth Legion," he said, suddenly cheerful.

The three of them laughed, delighted, and Or and Ayala introduced themselves as the children got to work with help from the rest of the team. Ayala spoke shyly, "Ms. Oshrat, you look more like your children's older sister than their mother."

Oshrat swelled with pride at such lavish praise. Ayala wasn't wrong; the woman was graceful and attractive, maybe around forty-five, Or guessed. She had youthful features; wavy blonde hair; clear, pale skin; and a slim, taut figure.

"Well, that's an exaggeration," Oshrat said, feigning embarrassment as she twirled her golden strands around a finger.

Or teased her. "Come on, then, what's your secret? Tell us, so we can be siblings to all four of you."

She giggled. "Maybe the secret's got to do with our healthy lifestyle at the kibbutz . . . fresh air, daily exercise, and—most important—good food."

Or sighed resentfully, "Good food . . . what a dream! We've been here for more than a week, and all our meals are basically fast food."

Ayala murmured her assent: "You're so right; I feel like I'm getting old here."

They chatted for a while about the benefits of healthy food, and then Oshrat joined her children, who were enjoying the ambiance of the expedition, wowed by the excavation work and the artifacts—potsherds, spearheads, and arrowheads. When it was almost 1 P.M., the end of the expedition's workday, Or's skill and experience in excavation had still failed to make an impression on Oshrat, who he'd been hoping would throw him a lifeline from behind the impregnable walls of Megiddo. He felt like he was about to drown in the depths of this miserable pit.

Oshrat rounded up her children and got them ready to go, expressing her sincere thanks to David and the team members for their hospitality and for looking out for her and the kids. As she was about to head to the bus, she turned back to Or and Ayala, driven by her motherly, god-fearing kibbutz heart, and said to them, "How would you two like to have lunch at my house sometime? Whenever you're free?"

Ayala heard the earnestness in Oshrat's voice and said, abashed, "Oh, we were just joking with you, Ms. Oshrat; the food in Mishmar HaEmek is good."

Or whispered in Nur's ear irritatedly, "Tell that Sephardic simpleton to shut up; she's going to ruin your good luck."

Or grinned and said, "Why not? I really miss good home-cooked meals and a family atmosphere. What do you think, Ayala?"

Embarrassed, she shrugged in agreement. Or continued: "Next Friday is our day off. Does that work for you, Ms. Oshrat?"

"Of course! I'll see you then."

They exchanged numbers, planning to meet up again on Friday at Kibbutz Megiddo.

* * *

[FRIDAY NIGHT – MAY 7:
THE WELL OF MISK AL-ATTAR IS MAGDALENE'S WELL]

The opportunity to visit the Megiddo settlement was another good sign from Magdalene; it strengthened my narrative approach and its fictional premise, which has started to lean more toward realism . . . After Ayala and I had lunch at Oshrat's house (and I can't lie, it was delicious, all kinds of seafood), I went for a walk through the settlement with Ayala and Oshrat and her children. I tried as hard as I could to play the role of the Ashkenazi archeologist as I examined some of the ruins, which were none other than the rubble of the ill-fated Al-Lajjun, until finally I stumbled across the well. What surprised—almost shocked—me was finding the remains of an Islamic shrine next to it. The shrine was built over a round stone, so I assumed it must be the Mosque of Abraham; Yaqut al-Hamawi mentions it in his literary geography, *Mu'jam al-Buldan*, or "Dictionary of Lands." As I examined the stones of the mosque, I imagined it was the shrine of Misk al-Attar, the grandson of Simon the Lame, who was Mary Magdalene's secret follower; I could almost smell the bewitching scent of nard emanating from the depths of the well, knowing that the village ruins were hidden by the lofty trees planted by the settlers in Megiddo. As for the well, I stood beside it, unable to see the bottom. Being with Ayala and Oshrat meant I couldn't let my imagination run totally wild, either as a writer or as an archaeologist, so I pulled myself together, consoling myself with the possibility of discovering the well's secrets later, in better circumstances, especially if I managed to win the affection of Oshrat and her children. No matter what, though, this initial discovery was a comfort. Now I have most of the material I need for my protagonist, Naseem Shakr. So I'm happy.

PS: Murad, today was a triumph; I finally managed to infiltrate Al-Lajjun as Or Shapira. I walked right into a house in the Megiddo settlement, ate delicious food, and chatted in Ashkenazi with a beautiful Zionist woman. When I politely inquired after the man of the house, she lit up with pride and said that her husband was a fighter pilot who'd gone to his air base a few days ago, and that he wouldn't be back anytime soon. She complained to me about the deteriorating security situation and the imminent threat to Israel from Hezbollah, Hamas, Iran, and Syria. She said she hadn't seen her husband much lately because the military bases were on heightened alert in case of impending war.

Don't swear at me, Murad, please . . . Let me finish. It wasn't me sitting with Ayala at Oshrat's table; it was Or. He's the one who consoled her, saying that every Zionist is proud of their army and air force, and he's the one who brought out the air force slogan, "The Best to Fly." That's what he said to her, totally oblivious to the rustling of the trees around him, weighed down by the fates of the villagers in doomed, depopulated Al-Lajjun. And Ayala, who cursed Arabs' very existence, their "terrorism," their presence around her, wasn't the tiniest bit afraid of the slight tremor of stonework beneath her, which used to be people's homes. Do you see what I mean, Murad?

Anyway, a few days ago, I almost ripped off the Or Shapira mask when I said good morning to Sama' Ismail in Arabic. I wished her good morning like they do in Haifa, with all the beauty of the Arabic phrase, would've wished her seven golden waves breaking in the sea of Haifa, too. So yes, she caught me by surprise, then attacked me, the alleged Or. I don't have her deep-rooted ideas and national identity, so I couldn't respond. How was I supposed to respond? For God's sake, Murad, who even was I in that moment? Or or Nur?

Now I can also tell you, and only you, that I was disturbed by how comfortable she was speaking to me as Or Shapira. Isn't that normalization?!

Or does the fact that she's forced to live in daily conflict with the Zionist Other justify her ability to talk to Or like that, so frankly? And what about me? I don't know . . . My annoyance quickly subsided, though, when I noticed a tattoo on the inside of her pale, slender arm . . . a small, captivating tattoo, a song of perseverance and survival: Haifa 1948.

CHAPTER 7

It was a quiet afternoon threaded through with gentle breezes, draped over the sprawling space between the deep exhale of a plain and the sigh of a mountain, whose forested edge twitched slightly as a band of hikers climbed its rocky, pine-covered shoulder.

It was Saturday, a day of rest and relaxation for the expedition members. Or's team was now climbing the slope of the mountain with Natan Khodrovsky, the Mishmar HaEmek security guard, leading the way. Before the hike began, he'd asked Or for help with translation, in case his English failed him as he introduced the team members to the main facilities of the settlement. Or had agreed, saying he'd be proud to carry out the task of translating for these foreigners, who would soon head home with new knowledge about both their discoveries on the dig and the Zionist virtues that enveloped the kibbutz.

Nur had accepted his supervisor David Adams' invitation to join them on this hike around the settlement and its forest, during which they would visit Mishmar HaEmek's historical landmarks. David had emphasized the word "historical," which Nur didn't love, just as he didn't love this time, a time that wasn't his, dominating a place that *was* his not so long ago, before the Nakba and refugeehood. Now he was just a tourist in this labyrinth, a colonial labyrinth, as Murad would describe it. What was he doing here? There was a false note in the rhythms of justification and consolation he kept pace with, a tightrope walker with Nur and Or together in his arms, afraid of falling into the laughter of this place that was closing in on him. Maybe the thing suffocating him was the mask, Or Shapira's mask.

"For heaven's sake, then, why did you agree to go on this hike?"

"I want to understand who you all are at the core—what it is that got you a state."

"Aren't you sick of the getting-to-know-you phase? Look around; it's clear. Not a miracle at all."

"Total clarity is frightening . . . The brightness hides a kind of darkness."

"We're a light for you . . . a light unto the nations. We came to this land when it was in ruins, to fix it. Did you know the kibbutz and the lands around it used to be swamps? Full of disease and filth."

"Swamps are more beautiful than settlements."

"You're so backward and primitive . . . and bitter."

"Why, thank you, O civilized, enlightened one."

"I'll blow your cover."

"I'll blow yours first."

He walked alongside David and Natan, who had turned in a twinkling from a security guard into the group's tour guide. They were one team member short; Ayala had opted to spend the weekend with her family in the Ramat Gan settlement, giving Nur a break from the burden of her constant irritation with Sama'. The latter, who had also decided to spend the weekend away, in Haifa, and would be back to work the next day, was the one he missed. The real reason he was taking part in this hike, though, was the euphoria he felt after visiting the ruins of Al-Lajjun the day before, a Magdalene coincidence having lit his path to the well of Misk al-Attar. Imagination possessed him, floored him, and he found himself in a mysterious land somewhere between reality and fantasy, hopes and facts, dreams and events. He'd subjugated his vision for the novel to another one that was more realistic, inspecting the remains of this village rooted in history and trying to derive from its stones the truth of his existence there—and not just truth but legitimacy, one that justified his presence in that settlement, as Or and as Nur. It was a settlement that had taken over the expanse of time and space in an asymmetry that made it sublime, transcending what the country had suffered of occupation and conflagration, centers and margins, and this expanse gripped him so that he, too, could rise above the bleeding wounds he'd left behind in Jerusalem, where he had roamed so recently, Nur through her alleyways and Or through her streets.

How he missed Jerusalem! Especially after making his rounds of online news that morning and discovering that tensions had escalated even higher in the city's public spaces because of the settlers' continued incursions into the Al-Aqsa compound, and that more and more people were showing solidarity with the Sheikh Jarrah residents threatened with eviction. How could he comment on that news here? What would he say to the members of his team following Natan, light unto the nations, who was guiding them around the main landmarks of this "historical kibbutz"?

"Our kibbutz was founded in 1926 by the HaShomer HaTzair movement, by some immigrants who made aliyah from Poland. It is one of the few kibbutzim—"

He leaned over to Or and asked him shyly in Hebrew to translate the rest of his speech. Biting back Nur's impulse to groan, Or continued for him: "Mishmar HaEmek is one of the few kibbutzim that hasn't given in to privatization. Its economic and social structure is still socialist, so all the factories and workshops we visited are collectively owned by the kibbutz members."

Natan interrupted him, saying with Ashkenazi pride, "And here is Palmach Cave, the most important site in the kibbutz and the War of Independence."

They trickled into the large, spacious cave, equipped as

befits a historical tourist attraction with lights, informational pamphlets in different languages, and some plaques and photographs hanging on its rocky walls. As the team members looked around at the cave and its contents, eyes round with curiosity and wonder, Natan took up his commentary again in faltering English. "During World War II—in 1942, specifically—people were afraid Germany would win, and—"

Or came to his rescue again as he continued in Hebrew: "In 1942, after the Nazis had a series of victories, the British army transformed the kibbutz into a training camp for more than a hundred and sixty Jewish volunteers. They were trained to build explosives and operate and sabotage wireless communications systems, and they hid tons of explosives around the kibbutz, including in this cave. Once the Nazi threat was gone, those trainees joined the Palmach, the Haganah's strike force, which turned this cave into a training site and secret meeting place."

Natan interrupted him, proudly adding in English, "The cave played a decisive role in beating back the Arab attack on the kibbutz during the War of Independence, and was an important foothold during the counterattack launched by the Palmach and Haganah against Arab militias."

Natan's sudden fluency in English threw Nur off balance. For a moment, he wondered if Natan was so proud of this information that he'd memorized that last paragraph in English, which made Or whisper sarcastically in Nur's ear: "If only *you* were that fluent in Ashkenazi! Why do you have to make me look bad—why didn't you jump in there to explain?"

"I would've made you look worse if I'd decided to tell these people—so fascinated by your socialist Zionist paradise!—that the kibbutz is built on top of a village called Abu Shusha, which was destroyed in the Nakba. Or that this cave from your sacred nationalist texts was just a playground for kids from a depopulated village, and a pen for their livestock."

"All lies . . .! You're delusional."

"And you're finally starting to see your real face in the mirror . . ."

They exited the cave with fragments of the legend Natan had told them slung over their backs like arrows in a quiver and set out to climb the mountain, heading deep into the vast forest. Natan informed them that the Israel Land Fund and the early kibbutz residents had planted most of this forest after the War of Independence so that the future children of Israel could enjoy the steppes and greenery that were now their reality. One of the Belgian women, Nicole, leaned against a huge pine tree and asked him, "What about these stones, Mr. Natan? They look like the remains of houses, don't you think?"

Nur was so grateful for the question, which hit at the Achilles' heel of Natan's claims, that he almost hugged her, but the latter promptly dismissed her surprise, answering confidently, "These are ancient ruins, motek. Or have you forgotten you're in the land of the Torah and the Old Testament?"

Her expression only darkened. "Have you forgotten I'm an archaeologist? I can tell whether these stones are Biblical or the ruins of an Arab village that was depopulated during your 'War of Independence.' Sama' confirmed as much."

Nur tried with all his might to hide his feelings and emote a scowling solidarity worthy of Or as Natan issued his denial. "We didn't depopulate anything. Some of the original inhabitants fled at the height of the fighting and never came back. What Sama' said doesn't necessarily reflect the truth of what happened here."

Or spoke up in Hebrew to spare the group a conversation that was getting tense, addressing Natan. "Enough of Sama's nonsense for now, Natan. Let's head back . . . It's getting late, and there are wolves in this forest, remember?"

Natan agreed, trying to suppress his extreme irritation at Nicole for spoiling his Zionist panegyric with questions that smacked of Sama's Haifa accent. Nicole took Emily's arm as they hiked back down to the settlement, whispering in a low growl that she wasn't convinced: "There's a huge difference between migration and forced displacement."

* * *

[SATURDAY EVENING – MAY 8]

The sixth angel poured out his bowl on the great river Euphrates, and its water was dried up, to prepare the way for the kings from the east. And I saw, coming out of the mouth of the dragon and out of the mouth of the beast and out of the mouth of the false prophet, three unclean spirits like frogs. For they are demonic spirits, performing signs, who go abroad to the kings of the whole world, to assemble them for battle on the great day of God the Almighty. ("Behold, I am coming like a thief! Blessed is the one who stays awake, keeping his garments on, that he may not go about naked and be seen exposed!") And they assembled them at the place that in Hebrew is called Armageddon.

Revelation 16: 12-16

Holy night terrors, not even the most creative film directors could turn a vision like that into a movie. Or, well, maybe that's too hasty a judgment . . . James Cameron, or Peter Jackson, who directed *The Lord of the Rings*, might be able to manage it. It would be riveting—and terrifying.

PS: Murad, I know my apology for what I did today won't be enough for you. Trust me, I know . . . You have every right to rip out my heart and scrub at it to remove the godforsaken leech that sucked my blood and turned me into an expert Zionist translator. You have every right to perform some ritual to exorcize my demons, the demons of Mary Magdalene that seem to have possessed me.

But Nicole's question—honed by her conversations with Sama' about the Nakba—made the job of translating a little less bitter. It dealt a decisive blow to Natan's attempts to falsify history, to transform the settlement into a kibbutz, the swamp into paradise, the cave into an empty space, the graveyard into a forest and the tombstones into rocks, and the echoes of wails that still cling to the tree branches into shouts of victory.

During our hike in the forest, I got goosebumps from the rustling and the smell of pine Or was inhaling. But personally, once Nicole spotted the ruins of Abu Shusha, what I smelled was death. It made me think of a talk by the Israeli novelist A.B. Yehoshua at a symposium about his narrative discourse, which he himself viewed as controversial. Don't act so surprised, Murad—yes, I attended that symposium. It was held at one of the cultural centers in West Jerusalem, and I went as Or Shapira, though not as openly as I've taken on the persona since. Anyway, I won't bore you with the details . . . But while I was walking under those trees, I remembered what the novelist had said about the criticism he got for his novella about the forests planted to hide the ruins of Arab villages from '48. In the book, the Palestinian protagonist living there has had his tongue cut out, which makes it impossible for him to reveal what the forest contains in its verdant folds. I remember Yehoshua saying, "If I'd given him a tongue, he would've given voice to the secrets of the forest instead of burning it to reveal the destroyed village. I didn't want him to speak but to act, by burning the forest."

Honestly, Murad, I wanted to ask him, *Why didn't you show the village being destroyed in the novel? Why didn't you address the ethnic cleansing?* I realize now how valid it is to ask those questions of a writer who's tackling history from a Zionist platform and whose fiction is laden with facts.

At any rate, I wouldn't have burned the forest I was hiking through as a translator and tourist . . . I would've liked to burn myself and my mask instead . . . Who knows, maybe I would rise from the ashes more like Sama'. Sama' Ismail . . .

* * *

He crept along quietly, clad in the obscurity of a pitch-black night, through the dense underbrush, retracing his steps from when he'd visited the ruins of the destroyed village of Al-Lajjun as Or Shapira. Now, he was Nur, Nur al-Shahdi, and he'd managed to penetrate the walls of the Megiddo settlement and was heading toward its southeastern edge, which held the thing he craved in its embrace, his vision manifested as a well.

He stopped next to this well with no moon at its bottom, no moon in the sky above. He made sure the night was still, nothing lurking to attack his devotion to Magdalene, then opened his gear bag and took out a sturdy rope, knotting one end around a rock next to the well. He yanked on the rope to test it, his chest heaving excitedly, then took a deep breath and dropped into the well, bracing his legs against its cylindrical wall. It wasn't very deep, which surprised him. When his feet touched bottom, where a small amount of brackish water had collected, he took out a flashlight and a slender chisel to inspect the well wall.

Carefully, skillfully, he scraped and tapped against it with the chisel, hoping to hear a hollow thud indicating a void. Nothing. Before the frustration could get to him, he knelt down, repeating the onslaught more vigorously this time, until he heard the sound he'd been waiting for, something different, the sound of an empty space behind the part of the wall he was working on. He renewed his efforts, scraping harder. Certain now that there was a concealed niche, he looked for an edge or corner, and finally the chisel sank halfway into the wall. He stifled a howl. He set about widening the space around the edge until the niche appeared, no more than sixty centimeters square. He gasped for breath, panting as he succeeded in loosening its cover. He put the end of the flashlight between his teeth and used his knife and chisel, one in each hand, to pry it off. After a few moments of straining, he succeeded.

He sprang up, trembling from the sudden shock and breathing hard. Then he pulled himself together, feeling an almost magnetic pull from the water seeping toward the void, deep inside the niche. He crawled steadily, confidently, for several meters inside a dark, narrow tunnel that led him to another empty space, this one bigger: a long, slender corridor that allowed him to stand upright. He edged forward with caution, then stopped abruptly when he saw a door at the end of the corridor with seven blazing torches mounted above it. He turned off his flashlight to make sure he wasn't imagining the light emanating from them, then advanced in a rush of excitement until he heard echoed whispers and chants coming from behind the door. His heart pounded violently, terror crept into his limbs, and he froze in place. Then he pressed forward again, peering into a large, domed room filled with glowing lanterns and the sweet scent of nard. In its center, a crowd was gathered around a human figure clad in a loose white silk robe, made all the more enchanting by the lustrous black curls that cascaded across its cheeks and down its shoulders. A soft, feminine voice emanated from it, whispering a chant that Nur could not understand. The scent of the perfume intoxicated him, as did the rhythms of the circle, which was made of up a few dozen men and women he assumed were followers of the figure sitting cross-legged at its center.

He was staring intently, trying to make out the figure's features, when it suddenly raised its head. The woman gathered her curls behind her back and stared at him with a face that Nur al-Shahdi knew well. A tremor ran through him. She looked like Sama' Ismail. She opened her mouth wide and a bright white light emerged from deep inside, flowing toward him and pushing him away, forcing him down, out of the atmosphere of the circle, the corridor, the niche, and the bottom of the well, ejecting him from the luminous moment as he clung to his final cry, which rang out as he emerged from slumber.

* * *

He was drained after a hard day's work with very little rest. He was sitting next to Ayala on the bus, which had nearly arrived at Mishmar HaEmek, carrying the expedition members back from the dig.

He'd been distracted for two days, infatuated, completely zoned out, and occasionally cranky; he hadn't gotten much sleep since the dream, whose light was still coursing forward into the present moment, something that made Or's blood boil. He whispered, "What's your problem? You've been annoying as hell ever since the night before last. Where did you go? Tell me!"

"I was in a dream. I'm alone when I dream—you're not there."

"What was the dream about?"

"My wildest hopes . . . "

Ayala snapped him out of his silent conversation with Or, trying again to improve his mood, which had been sour since the morning: "There's going to be a huge demonstration in Jerusalem tomorrow. They'll raise the Israeli flag to prove to the Arabs that it's Yerushalayim and not Al-Quds. That the Temple Mount is ours."

He responded with listless indifference: "The situation's already tense; a demonstration like that will only make things worse . . . "

"What are you talking about? The Arabs need to get it through their heads that Jerusalem's under Israeli sovereignty, all of it. Saying stuff like that will only make them greedier; they'll think it's rightfully theirs."

The bus arrived at the settlement, and he got off, remarking dryly, "Then I hope our Jewish sovereignty demonstration ends well."

She followed him toward the dining hall along with the other expedition members and sighed. "You know what? You're annoying as hell when you're tired."

"I know . . . I know."

He let her go on ahead, sneaking a furtive glance at Sama' as she went to her room on the second floor of the main building to rest. She was still fasting during this holy month that he'd long ago abandoned. It was her—it definitely was. She was still shining after his dream, still part and parcel of his passion for Mary Magdalene.

She crossed in front of him, near him, or rather through him, like a soft, gentle wave, saturated with inner calm.

In the dining hall, he opted to sit with Nicole and Emily, avoiding Ayala's resentment and hurtful comments about Nur and Sama's shared roots.

He ate with them, talking over the day's big accomplishments at the excavation site, where they'd found traces of the camp's main street in addition to water drainage channels and Roman military equipment including helmets, shields, and spears, which lent a cheery atmosphere to the expedition. But at a time when Brian, Peter, and David should've been overjoyed by the achievement, they were, instead, morose and discontent. Nur was positive that their glumness came from their complete failure to find some specific thing in the depths of the dig site. He had confirmed this belief when he approached them as they held a whispered conversation next to the tent, pretending to busy himself arranging potsherds in boxes. Brian was complaining. "Well, damn it . . . I guess we're looking in the wrong place."

He was about to continue whispering to his two colleagues when he noticed Or there, pretending to be sorting through the pottery. He'd signaled to David and Peter to move away from the tent toward a far corner of the site that Nur's eyes and ears couldn't reach.

Nur finished his meal and said goodbye to Emily and Nicole, then headed for his room to wash up and get some rest. That rest had been refusing to come to him since he'd come to the settlement, all mask and mirrors, and now that he'd given up on it, there was no possible escape other than recording a new voice memo that might alleviate his fatigue and anxiety.

[Monday Afternoon – May 10]

Murad, I can't seem to keep up with Magdalene's story here, in this especially troubled corner of our homeland. I don't know what's happening to me! I feel drained dry, especially after the dream (or vision?) I had two days ago. It felt so real, Murad! Like I could reach out and touch her. She was luminous . . .

That's the thing that worries me. I mean—if I have such a top-tier imagination, textured so much like the truth, then what am I doing? Why am I here? Isn't it about time I moved on, leaving my quest and this mask behind?

* * *

After they finished classifying and cleaning their archaeological finds in the lab, they headed to the conference room for a lecture called "The Question of Solomon's Stables," presented by David Adams.

Once they'd settled in, Brian stepped up to the podium to announce to the audience that special guests from the kibbutz had been invited to the lecture. He gestured toward the front row in welcome.

They were three men and two women, all elderly survivors of the Shoah, the horrible Nazi Holocaust. Brian introduced them solemnly, in a voice brimming with sympathy. Memory and death were tattooed on their arms in the form of the serial numbers they'd been branded with in the death camps of Auschwitz, Dachau, Birkenau, and others.

David opened his lecture by extending his own welcome to these special guests, then proceeded to review the arguments in favor of the historicity of the Tel Megiddo stables, discovered a few years prior. Archaeological research indicated that they dated back to the early Iron Age, the beginning of the tenth century BC, which was the golden age of King Solomon. According to that logic, the stables had to be Solomon's, which also proved that he existed. Then David discussed the opposing arguments, which not only denied the attribution of the stables to Solomon, but the ruler's historical existence, as well.

The lecture was short. David wrapped it up by declaring that he didn't want to offer any definitive answers; he would leave that to the historians and archaeologists specializing in this mysterious period.

As the audience dispersed after the lecture, each person back to his or her own affairs, a small crowd remained around the five Holocaust survivors, listening with reverence and sympathy to their stories of death. Nur didn't join them at first; he was too busy exchanging messages with Sheikh Morsi, checking in on him, especially given the difficulties Jerusalem was facing.

When he looked up from his phone, Sama's presence in the group immediately caught his attention. It was touching, the way she listened to the survivors' stories with genuine empathy. For the first time in his life, Nur al-Shahdi asked himself, *What is my position on the Holocaust?*

Or emerged suddenly and whispered his own question: "What did you say?!"

"What is my position on the Holocaust? What do I think about the camps, the gas chambers?"

"Is that an actual question?"

"Yes."

"Why?"

"Because I'm living in my own gas chamber."

"Don't you dare compare your tragedy to ours. Do you hear me?"

Fresh from this altercation with Or, he joined some of the other expedition members, moved by the five guests who were now filing out of the building to return to their homes in the settlement. The circle of sympathy that had enfolded them was replaced by a heated argument outside the dining room, Ayala heaping insults on Sama' as dinnertime approached. The others gathered around them, taken aback by this guttural argument in Hebrew, understanding nothing but the tension and anger brewing between the two women. Or hurried into the tumult with no idea how to resolve their argument. Ayala was seething. "You spiteful bitch—how the hell can you accuse Israel of 'committing a holocaust' against you? I heard you slandering us in front of the foreigners."

Sama' was incensed. "The ethnic cleansing you carried out against us is the definition of a holocaust."

Ayala took a step toward her and said angrily, "Instead of expressing sympathy for these survivors, you're accusing them of committing a shoah against you?!"

"No, I'm expressing sympathy and solidarity with victims of the Nazi Shoah, but based on my own understanding of it, not your Zionist one."

"Okay, bitch, how do you understand it?"

"You called me spiteful, but you're the spiteful one. You're too blinded by your spite to acknowledge the facts."

"What facts? The state of Israel's the only fact you need to acknowledge, whether you like it or not."

"Screw you . . . I'm still here, and I'm not going anywhere. There's your fact."

Fuming, Ayala was about to hurl herself at Sama' when David grabbed her hand and pulled her gently away, wanting to put an end to this noisy argument in Hebrew, of which he'd understood nothing except the terrifying word "holocaust." Meanwhile, Or just stood there with his arms folded, doing nothing, because Nur wanted to stand with Sama' and Or with Ayala. Instead, muddled, he kept his mouth shut.

The small crowd dispersed after Sama' turned and stormed out of the building. Nur hurried after her as David offered Ayala a cigarette to calm her down.

This time, Nur didn't hesitate. He went outside, where he glimpsed her standing next to a bushy cypress across from the building. Evening's translucent darkness had settled over the landscape, blending into the empty streets and squares of the kibbutz. He walked toward Sama' without her noticing; she was looking off in the direction of the mountain, her back to the building as Nur approached, her muffled sobs reaching his ears. When she heard the sound of his footsteps, she turned, startled, and quickly wiped her tears away, surprised by his sudden appearance. She said to him in Hebrew, her husky voice sharp, "What do *you* want? Are you here to tell me how spiteful I am, too? Accuse me of antisemitism?"

He stopped a few steps away. He was out of breath, shivering. He mumbled for a few moments, stuttering out a few semi-words, and then said, with all the Arabic he had in him: "Sama', I'm not Jewish. I'm Arab, like you . . ."

She took an involuntary step back and bumped into the tree trunk, shocked by the sudden confession in Arabic. "What?" She was stammering, still in Hebrew. "Are you messing with me or something? Is this some dirty Israeli game?"

His Arabic was wounded, pleading: "No, please believe me . . . I'm an Arab Palestinian refugee, and I live in a camp in Ramallah. I'm originally from Al-Lydd."

"Stay where you are—don't come near me. Have you lost your mind? What are you babbling about? And where did you learn Arabic? Are you Shin Bet?"

He managed a whisper. "No. Please speak to me in Arabic. My name is Nur . . . Nur Mahdi al-Shahdi, not Or Shapira."

She stared at him for a few moments, trying to compose herself, then said, cautiously, in Arabic, "How is that possible? Everything about you screams Ashkenazi Jew. Do you think I'm stupid enough to believe you . . .? I know Shin Bet agents are fluent in Arabic."

"What would the Shin Bet want with this expedition and its ruins?"

"What do *you* want with it?"

"I'm writing a novel on Mary Magdalene. It takes place here on this plain, in the village of Al-Lajjun. And I can't come here with my Palestinian ID, so I'm using a Zionist identity."

"What kind of flimsy claim is that? A refugee working on a novel about Mary Magdalene?"

"Believe me . . . I can prove it. Or Shapira's just a mask . . . like your blue ID."

She came closer to him, defiant, her Arabic stern, "You moron, I've been waiting my whole life to be freed from this identity . . . and you, you threw your entire life away when you put on that mask. Having this ID has only made me unhappy."

She started back to her room and, when he blocked her path, yelled at him in Hebrew: "Get out of my way! You're either crazy, a normalizing traitor, or a Shin Bet officer. Choose whichever mask you want, but move!"

In the face of her outburst, he stepped aside, defeated. He lowered his head and turned to the cypress tree, then put his arms around it and wept in anguish.

* * *

[MONDAY NIGHT – MAY 10]

I'm not a traitor or a normalizer, and I'm not in the Shin Bet. What I might be is lost, crazy, or confused. That's how I was going to answer her, Murad . . . I nearly told her, "My name is Nur. Ask around about me—ask my friend Murad, Sheikh Morsi, the alleyways of the camp, my father's silence, my grandmother Sumayyah, my mother's grave . . . Ask Mary Magdalene." But she left, this woman who'd turned from a lush rose into a violent insurrection after I sprang my name and origin on her. I just couldn't stand there helpless anymore as Ayala insulted and scolded her. So I tore off my mask all at once and told her my secret, my story, and she cursed and yelled at me, refusing to have anything to do with me. But she's right, isn't she, Murad? She's right. Which is why I feel relieved now that I've confessed . . . It's the bitter end for this mask of mine. You might be wondering what's next—what's the next step? How will I face her tomorrow? Will I wear my mask to the dig? Will I try talking to her in front of the Zionists and foreigners, broadcasting the fact that I'm an Arab refugee?

I don't know . . . Mostly, what I know now is that I draw courage from her, and hope and certainty. Especially after seeing her face off against Ayala about the most untouchable doctrine in Zionism, the Shoah. Sama' had the guts to express solidarity with the victims of the Holocaust from a humanitarian standpoint, not a Zionist one. I understood what she meant. She's against Zionism co-opting the Shoah, turning it into a moral system that protects and legitimizes the ethnic cleansing practiced against us during the Nakba. In that moment of sympathy and solidarity, I wanted to shout at the crowd around the five Holocaust survivors and ask, *Ladies and gentleman, what's the difference between the numbers tattooed on your arms and the tattoo on Sama's: "Haifa 1948"?*

It's an existential difference. It's cause and effect. If the Holocaust hadn't happened, Sama' wouldn't have tattooed her arm like that. She would've tattooed a butterfly, a flower, a wave . . . I nearly shouted, *What's the difference between Nazi gas chambers and a traffic light?*

There isn't one. Both inventions were born from the same womb: modernity. Right, Murad? At least, that's what I read in one of your books; I think it was *Modernity and the Holocaust*, by Zygmunt Bauman. Right?

When I confided in her about Magdalene and why I was here, she mocked me the way you always do. A Palestinian escapes the alleyways, the camp, the Occupation, and all the attendant hardships to write a novel responding to Dan Brown and *The Da Vinci Code*. What kind of bullshit is that? What navel-gazing nonsense?

So now I'm discovering, more than ever, that Sama' Ismail is the luminous Mary Magdalene. And me? Well, whoever I am, it's not Jesus. Maybe I'm Judas Iscariot.

No, don't swear at me . . . I said what I said: Judas Iscariot. Without him, Jesus would never have become the redeemer and savior.

* * *

The next day, the world drew its brightness not from the midday sun but from Nur's own nakedness at the excavation site.

At least that's how he felt as he threw himself into work in the team's test pit, seeking to bury his nakedness in the dirt of yesteryear, trying not to look toward Sama', who every now and then would glare over at him, her eyes flashing with astonishment and confusion at what he'd told her the night before. She was the sky, farther away than ever from Nur, who'd hit rock bottom in the pit of identity, the identity of the Other, which he was now trying to tear himself away from by making that final confession to Sama'.

Despite his boundless energy for digging, cleaning, and marking sections of the pit, he was pale and distracted. His team members noticed this extra effort and asked him more than once to take a rest; they still had plenty of time to find and extract the pit's secrets.

During the second break, only Ayala was brave enough to approach him and check in, surprised by how absorbed he was in his work. "What's up, why are you working like you're about to find buried treasure?"

He feigned a smile, dazzling her: "That's exactly why; I'm about to find buried treasure."

"Okay, well, split it with me when you do."

"Naturally . . . "

He knew, deep down, that she would strike now, shifting from her calm, good-natured mood to a state of agitation, and that she would snap at him. Why hadn't he stood by her yesterday during the argument with Sama'? And where did he disappear to when she needed him?

She didn't disappoint. He responded to the onslaught with Ashkenazi poise: "Ayala, I'm sick of the endless arguments between you two. And honestly? You don't need a defense attorney. You're capable of defending yourself, no?"

"But I needed you to translate, to show these foreigners she's antisemitic and completely obsessed with conflicts that happened ages ago—she just refuses to get over it . . . "

Brian's voice broke into their argument from a distance. "We've found the camp commander's headquarters! Come see."

The jubilant yell was enough to save him from Ayala's reproaches and the siege she'd laid with her expectations of

Zionist solidarity. He turned and headed toward the vast pit where Brian was standing, accompanied by a group of other expedition members, all of them gazing at a damaged stone archway, its keystone carved with the head of a winged ram, one of the most important pagan symbols in ancient Rome. Sama' stood there with them contemplating this important discovery, but, before long, she looked up at the edge of the pit where Nur was standing. He stepped back and ducked out of sight, shielding himself as much as possible from her sharp gaze.

* * *

[Tuesday Afternoon, May 11]

Murad, the horizons of my novel on Magdalene have gone dark and been replaced by the revelation of Sama'. The sky.

I'm miserable . . . A pile of desolate ruins.

By the way, Murad, did I ever tell you what the Hebrew word for mask is?

It's a lot like the English word "mask," both in the way it's pronounced and in its double meaning. "Masekhah." If we sprinkle a little Arabic on it, it would be "masekh," which, in Arabic, means a freak. A masekh is masekhah because he's mis-shapen. Me, I'm not wearing a mask; I'm wearing that other ugly shape. I actually am a freak, born from the womb of the Nakba, the confusion and alienation and silence: the silence of my father and the death of my mother . . . born from the camp's alleys where I was chased, the nickname Saknaji echoing after me . . . I was born from the womb of marginalization, classifi-cation, and your imprisonment, Murad. I was born from Or Shapira's mirror, from Shakib al-Qassabi's travel agency . . . I am the freak, my friend—is there any womb in the world that would bear me again, this time as a human being? Is there a sky in which I can find expression as Nur, as light and fire?

His voice was bitter as he finished recording, and he decided to head for the lab to get back to his daily duties, full of names and dates and other minutiae. Only a handful of expedition members were there when he arrived, absorbed in classifying and documenting the modest number of finds they'd extracted from the site that day. He busied himself cleaning potsherds with a brush. He loved these shards; they had so much to say about their ancient past. Every piece of pottery extracted from the earth got them closer to uncovering the fate and conditions of the dig site; it was an archive of the past that, without fail, recorded most of the events that had befallen a particular era.

Then Ayala came looking for him in the lab, puncturing his concentration. "Did you hear what's happening in Yerushalayim?"

"No . . . What's happening?"

Her breathing was shallow with emotion: "They're saying the Hamas terrorists have given our government until 6 P.M. to stop the flag march that's supposed to happen soon in the Old City."

Heart pounding, he feigned disapproval. "Hamas is giving the State of Israel an ultimatum?!"

"We won't give into those terrorists," she said, her voice shaking, "The government has announced that Jerusalem will remain in Jewish hands, and the Israeli flag will fly proudly throughout the whole country."

"Of course."

"Come on . . . Let's go to the conference room. Everyone's there in front of the big screen, waiting for six o'clock. Come on! It's seven till."

Or thought for a moment that she was joking, but one of his lab colleagues quickly dispelled that belief, saying that Brian had decided to push the six o'clock lecture to the next day because of the breaking news from Jerusalem. He jumped out of his chair and hurried with Ayala toward the conference room.

The atmosphere was fraught with suspense and trepidation, and most of the expedition members were packed into the room, staring intently at the projection screen where the Zionist channel 13 news was broadcasting live coverage of the heated events around Damascus Gate. The title they'd chosen for the news ticker at the bottom of the screen was sensational: "Hamas gives Israel 6 P.M. ultimatum."

Nur glanced around like he always did, looking for Sama', only to find her seeking him out, too. She was standing next to one of the students a few steps to his left. He felt she'd been waiting for him to arrive, to see his reaction to the developments in Jerusalem. He felt himself avoiding her eyes as Ayala, next to him, craned her neck to better see the screen. As the clock struck six, announcing the end of Hamas's deadline, a tense silence fell over the room. The seconds ticked by. Five . . . ten . . . fifteen seconds, followed by a violent blast. Sirens sounded in Jerusalem, warning of the imminent arrival of a salvo of rockets fired from Gaza.

The room filled with commotion, gasps of surprise and disapproving murmurs. He turned to his left, stealing a glance at Sama' without drawing Ayala's attention. The shadow of a smile had crept across her face; Nur caught it as she met his gaze for a few moments before turning abruptly to leave the conference room. Ayala sagged against Or, and he embraced her, consolatory: "It's all right, motek; they're just warning shots. They won't hit anyone."

She burst into tears, burying her wet face in his chest, then let out a strangled cry. "The damn terrorists have ruined the Jerusalem Day march."

Or stroked her back sympathetically as Nur tried to keep his head from exploding. It was all too much: the sound of the sirens, that smile Sama' had given him as she left the conference room . . .

He extricated himself from Ayala's arms and urged her, with all the Ashkenazi sympathy he could muster, to go to her room and get some rest, lifting his chin and adding firmly, "Our army will respond to this attack with massive attacks of their own. Don't worry, motek."

* * *

He drifted off to his room after more than an hour in the conference room, where he'd been following the latest developments broadcast by the Zionist news with interest. In spite of the ongoing coverage and the palpable sense of astonishment and agitation in the room, Sama' hadn't come back.

As soon as he threw himself onto his bed, Or emerged, fuming, "Happy now, you little

terrorist? You are, aren't you?"

"Why wouldn't I be?"

"So you support bombing innocent civilians and destroying their homes!"

"Oh, give it a rest; don't you ever get tired of repeating the same hypocritical talking points? Innocent people are being displaced from their homes in Sheikh Jarrah at this very moment using the weapon you've fashioned from sacred geography, and *your* bombs are about to set Gaza on fire."

"So we have nothing to say to each other."

"We do. I don't feed on the blood of innocent civilians on either side. I'm not a vampire."

"What do you mean?"

"Or . . . It's been three years since we first met in that flea market in Jaffa. What do you think of me now, especially after these last few days, when we've been forced to work so closely together?"

Silence.

"Answer me! Why are you so quiet?"

Silence.

"Don't you think I'm human, not just some nameless, featureless being, automatically classified as a terrorist or provocateur?"

"You only became a human being when we got here, and all thanks to me—to my identity."

"So if I took off your mask right now, I wouldn't be one anymore?"

Silence.

"Answer me, come on!"

"Okay . . . I don't know—maybe. I'm afraid that if you become human, I'll disappear."

"If you looked in the mirror right now, who would you see?"

"I'd see you."

"You'd see a human being."

He was brought out of his delirium by the ping of an incoming WhatsApp message on his cell phone.

Dear Expedition Members,

We regret to inform you that we are being required by the IDF's Home Front Command to halt work on the Sixth Legion site due to the tense security situation and the possibility of further missile fire, which could reach as far as the Jezreel Valley Regional Council kibbutzim.

Accordingly, the Albright Institute and Israel Antiquities Authority have opted to suspend this excavation season until further notice.

Please note that a final debriefing has been scheduled for tomorrow, Wednesday, May 12, at 9 A.M. in the conference room. This will be immediately followed by the departure of all expedition members from Kibbutz Mishmar HaEmek.

Sincerely,

Professor Brian Moore

General Supervisor, Second Excavation Season
Roman Sixth Legion Site

He finished reading the decision handed down by the institute and began to laugh so hard that the large mirror hanging opposite him on the bathroom wall shattered. Then he held the phone close to his mouth to record a new voice memo. He cleared his throat to speak before shaking his head gloomily and letting the phone fall onto the desk. He lay back, responding to the pull of sleep as the exterior Or was hidden away and the interior Nur was revealed.

* * *

The dew of silence wrapped itself around him, the silence of six in the morning, as he slipped quietly and cautiously out of his room with his big backpack. He left the dorm and was engulfed by the empty settlement. He looked around, taking in all the details: dorms, houses, lampposts, farms and factories, barns and silence. A basketball court alongside the slope of the mountain, whose rustling trees towered over the settlement. A partially destroyed monument and cars parked along the curb. Stillness.

Then he made his way out of this settlement and its time, which had been coursing through him for days. He reached the main gate and paused at the security booth, where Natan Khodrovsky, sensing his presence, momentarily let down his guard and jumped up from his chair to say good morning, commenting with a mix of sarcasm and earnestness, "I see you're in a hurry to go, Mr. Shapira. Have you been called up to join the reserves in case there's a war?"

Nur gave him a confident smile. "I'm ready any time."

"We all are."

They shook hands—a firm, friendly handshake to express

Or's gratitude for the warm welcome Natan and the kibbutz council had shown for the excavation project. Then Or bid the security guard farewell, turning right onto the shoulder of Highway 66. He'd walked just a few steps when Natan shouted after him, teasing, "Don't forget to renew your ID, Or Shapira!"

Or gave him a thumbs up in acknowledgement without looking back or worrying about his safety, even for a moment. He wasn't as afraid as he had been when he first entered the settlement; he was on his way out now, confident and reassured. *And I got what I wanted*, he thought.

The highway wasn't busy; it was a quiet morning, saturated with the calm of the Marj Ibn Amer valley and its fields. He walked slowly, his bag on his back and his head bowed to the ground as though rummaging through its depths, reflecting on the recent past he'd left behind him. He didn't turn around. He insisted on moving forward, even if he had no idea where he was headed.

He walked a few dozen meters like this, not noticing the white Hyundai that exited Mishmar HaEmek behind him until it veered right toward the shoulder, slowing and honking twice. He jumped, taking two steps back and freezing in place, stopping when the car did.

For a fleeting moment, he thought that Natan had figured out who he was. He started to compose himself, examining the car without registering the features of the person behind the wheel. Then the front passenger's side door flew open and a husky, feminine Palestinian voice issued from the figure inside. A cool, peaceful feeling descended over him. A feeling like the sky.

"Get in, you lunatic, I believe you; I've believed you since yesterday. I'm not going to leave you alone on this road when the whole country's burning. Come on—get in, Nur! What are you waiting for?"

He stood, stunned, in front of the open door, shrugged off his backpack, and bent over to look at Sama' Ismail, contemplating her for a moment—real, flesh-and-blood, no space left for a dream—then straightened up again. He removed the Star of David necklace from his chest, threw it as far as he could onto the plain beside the road, pulled the fake ID from his pocket, Or Shapira's ID, and showed it to Sama'. Then he ripped it apart and sent it after the necklace. He didn't say a word, but he could feel tears springing to his eyes. He took the phone out of his pocket, returned its settings to Arabic, put his bag in the back of the car, and gave a deep sigh. Gazing at her with feeling, he got in and pulled the door shut. Before they drove away, he whispered in his reclaimed Arabic, with every ounce of energy he possessed, "You are my identity; you're my destination."

* * *

Author's Note

November 9, 2021
The Colony's Gilboa Prison
The world of this novel would have been impossible without the attention and efforts of the excellent Dr. Johnny Mansour from Haifa, who provided me with information on the settlement of Mishmar HaEmek, the depopulated village of Al-Lajjun, the Bar Kokhba Revolt, and the excavation season for the Sixth Roman Legion with the Albright Institute. I alone bear the responsibility for how this material was handled.

I also extend my sincere thanks and appreciation to my brothers and fellow detainees from proud Jerusalem, who surrounded me with attention, information, and care. I would especially like to thank my friend Mamdouh Amireh, a graduate of the Institute of Islamic Archaeology at Al-Quds University whose valuable information transformed me into an archaeologist, and brother Sanad al-Tarman, who never ceased to amaze me with the precision of his observations, derived from his novelist's sense of the details and geography of Jerusalem.

Bassem

Bassem Khandaqji, born in 1983 in Nablus, is a Palestinian novelist, poet, and journalist. Arrested in 2004 at the age of twenty-one for his political activities, he continued to write from prison, producing a body of work that has earned wide recognition across the Arab world. His novels are known for their lyrical prose, meticulous research, and deep engagement with Palestinian history and memory. Today, Khandaqji is regarded as one of the most distinctive literary voices of his generation. International human rights observers have long criticised his arrest, trial, and imprisonment. He was released from prison in 2025, one year after *A Mask the Colour of the Sky* won the prestigious International Prize for Arabic Fiction.